# PARIS 75

Billy Morris

ISBN: 9798332558047

Print Edition

Copyright 2024 Billy Morris

All Rights reserved. No part of this book may be reproduced in any form without the prior permission of the author.

Paris 75 is a work of fiction. All characters are fictitious. Any similarity to real persons, living or dead, is entirely coincidental and not intended by the author. Where 'real-life' named individuals and events appear or are mentioned, the situations, opinions, history and dialogues relating to those persons are entirely fictional and are in no way intended to depict or reflect actual events or facts.

The author can be contacted at
BM.Author@outlook.com

Billy Morris was born in Leeds, Yorkshire in 1966. He left Leeds in the late 1990's and has lived and worked in Europe and USA. He now lives mainly in South-East Asia.

He wrote the first book in the 'Eighties Leeds' series, 'Bournemouth 90' in 2021.

The sequel 'LS92' was published in 2022 and the prequel LS65 in 2023.

'Birdsong on Holbeck Moor' was published in October 2022.

## Accents, Dialects and Pronunciation

LS65 is set in Leeds, a city in West Yorkshire in the North of England. The Leeds accent is quite distinct and can even vary slightly between different areas of the city. Including dialogue exactly as it would actually be spoken, would make this book unreadable for many people. However, there are certain fundamental elements of the Leeds accent which I felt needed to be reflected in the text, in order to maintain a level of authenticity in the characters' speech.

The most obvious is the dropping of the word 'the' before a noun. In Leeds 'the' will be replaced by what linguists call a glottal stop. Actors on TV often get this wrong by either missing out 'the' entirely, or pronouncing a 't' in its place. As a Leeds speaker, I can't even explain how to execute a glottal stop. Google tells me it's achieved by rapidly closing the vocal chords. I've no idea how you do that. If you want to hear an example, I suggest you listen to an interview with David Batty or Kalvin Phillips. They're both experts. In the book, a glottal stop to replace 'the' is denoted by an apostrophe ('). "We're going to the pub' therefore becomes "We're off to 'pub".

Owt, Nowt and Summat – Anything, nothing and something will usually be replaced by owt, nowt and summat by a native Leeds speaker. The pronunciation of these words is open to some debate, but based on my own experience, I would say that owt and nowt rhyme with 'coat', although I am aware that in some parts of the city, both words would rhyme with 'shout'. Summat is universally pronounced 'summert'.

I felt that dialect would become unrealistic in the context of the story without at least including the above substitutions and I hope this doesn't impact on your enjoyment of the book.

# Chapter 1

## Tuesday, 1 April 1975, Sheffield, England.

*New Terror Puts Rees on the Rack — Ulster secretary Merlyn Rees will hold crisis talks with his security chiefs after a weekend of violence which saw nine people killed in bombings and shootings in Belfast. Mr Rees's problem is how to stop the violence without jeopardising the IRA ceasefire which has so far held since February.*

"Good win that with half of 'team out. Them kids Stevenson and Liddell did alright." The young man muttered under his breath and glanced over his shoulder towards the corrugated roof of Bramall Lane stadium, as a distant roar carried on the night breeze.

"What was that?" His friend ran a finger through his feather-cut and glanced at the lamplit silhouette of a curtain-twitching pensioner on Shoreham Street.

"Fuck's sake, 'Blades have equalised. Hurry it up or we'll lose this lot."

Ahead of them, a blue transit van disgorged a squad of black overcoats, each officer pulling on leather gloves and crash helmets in advance of the game's end. The street was empty apart from the group of a dozen men walking with purpose ahead of them, and the young man felt confident enough to reach into the pocket of his denim jacket to retrieve a white silk scarf bearing the words 'Armfield's Aces.' He tugged at the slip knot and placed it loosely around his neck.

The two of them broke into a jog, and were fifteen feet behind the group when the young man called out to a kid of their own age walking at the back.

"Alright Max?"

The youth turned and noticed them for the first time. He had dark, shoulder length hair and was wearing flared pin-striped trousers with a ten button waist-band and patch-pockets. The rounded 'fly-away' collar of his shirt extended beyond the scoop-neck of his three-star tank top.

"Alright Col, where've you two just come from?"

"We were stood behind you lot in 'ground." The young men quickened their step as the youth carried on walking to keep pace with the main group.

"Didn't notice you when it kicked off at half time. Fucking hell, we were up against half of 'stand."

"We'd gone down for a Waggon Wheel. Never saw that." The young man lied unconvincingly. They'd seen the trouble brewing, noticed the Blades fans nodding and pointing, and had shuffled back through the crowd, distancing themselves from the explosion of violence which had followed.

"Got a right whack on 'head." The youth tilted his face sideways to display a swelling above his right eye as they walked. "Did you come on 'train then?"

"Yeah, you?"

The young man smiled and shook his head.

"Nah, mini-bus...with this lot. You know who they are don't you...who we are?"

The two newcomers shook their heads.

"The Asylum, LS9. You must have heard of us?"

"Aye, everyone has."

Clenching his fists to stop his hands shaking, the young man observed the group properly for the first time. Mostly men in their mid to late twenties supplemented by a handful of teenagers. No scarves or colours or customised butcher's coats. No soul bags or skinners paired with spray painted Docs. Their style was more suedehead and smoothie from a couple of years earlier, and they seemed to be dressed for a night out rather than a football trip. Most wore wide legged parallel trousers and 'Budgie' jackets, 'bumble bee' or rainbow-stripe scoop necked sweaters or tank tops, a couple sported half-belted leather jackets. Some of the younger members wore black baseball boots or trainers by Gola or Adidas but most of the footwear was leather and smart rather than casual, striped Solatios and Royal brogues with heavy platform soles.

At the head of the group was a large man, the oldest present, six foot three and weighing seventeen or eighteen stone, wearing a sheepskin jacket. Next to him, striding out at the front was the obvious leader. Late twenties, with wavy, dark, collar length hair, wearing a navy polo-neck sweater beneath a knee length, black leather trench coat. He looked back at his friends, a confident, mischievous smile betraying the anticipation of imminent violence. A pirate commander proudly observing his crew.

"Better get rid of that if you're joining us." The youth nodded towards the silk scarf hanging from the young man's neck. "What are you? A fucking Christmas tree?"

The young man felt his face redden under the orange street lamp, and hurriedly stuffed the scarf into the pocket of his patch-covered denim jacket.

"Looks like we've got company lads." The man in the black leather trench coat spoke with a Scottish accent, and raised a gloved hand as the group paused at a busy road facing a graveyard.

A thickset man in a British Steel donkey jacket stood smiling in front of the church. He waved his arms above his head, and the young man wondered if he was the local madman, conducting an invisible choir, but quickly he realised. The man was signalling, summoning reinforcements from the streets beyond the church, from where dozens of pairs of legs now appeared, moving at speed towards them.

"Fucking hell!" The young man instinctively took a step back but the youth standing alongside him grabbed the sleeve of his denim jacket.

"Don't run. First rule. Asylum never run."

The Leeds group began to button up their jackets and pull on gloves. The man in the trench coat stood at the front of the group grinning, his dark eyes flashing with excitement.

"Stand Leeds. Let 'em come. And remember, never a step back!"

The Sheffield group numbered around forty, the leaders a dozen or so men in their mid-twenties, moving forward quickly, showing no fear. Behind them were mostly teenagers, some faces smiling, excited, others nervous, hesitating, their pace slowing as they realised this Leeds group weren't retreating.

"Come on then!" A roar from the group signalled the charge and they bounced forward towards the advancing Blades fans. The young man gasped for breath and felt his heart pounding in his chest, then turned to see his friend sprinting back across the road in the direction they'd come from.

He swallowed hard and felt his feet slip on the grass, looking down to see dog shit smeared up the side of his Doc Martens, then glanced up just as a fist smashed into his nose.

"No! I'm not with them! No, help..."

He sank to his knees as the metallic, salty taste of blood filled his mouth. He covered the back of his head and curled into a ball as he felt a platform heeled shoe repeatedly connect with his ribs. The sounds of violence raged around him for what seemed like hours, until the beating ended suddenly, and after a minute, he slowly lifted his head.

A youth in a leather jacket was lying prostrate on a grassy bank and an older man in an NCB donkey jacket was doubled over, spitting blood and teeth onto the stone-flagged path of the church. Beyond them the rest of the Sheffield fans were retreating, some backing away slowly with arms raised, goading the Leeds fans. Most were running fast with heads down, not daring to look back.

The young man grimaced with pain as he hauled himself upright, holding his ribs and blowing snotty blood from his nostrils. He sensed a presence behind him and glanced upwards, as the man in the leather trench coat strode past him towards the fleeing Blades fans.

"Come on then you fuckers! Who fancies a bit of this?"

He could hear the man breathing heavily and talking quietly to himself as he reached into his coat, then raised his arm skywards, a dark object extended in his right hand.

Spitting blood onto the grass, the young man kept his head down, and heard the man laughing as he walked past him again, but glanced up in time to see him slide a sawn-off shotgun back into the lining of his trench coat.

"You alright Col? Saw you getting a bit of a kicking there. I'd have helped you out but I had my hands full." The youth with the dark hair approached, rubbing at a lump over his eye and spitting bloody saliva onto swollen knuckles.

"Who is he?" The young man nodded at the man in the trench coat.

The youth shook his head and failed to stifle his laughter.

"You don't know who that is? That's Mad Alan. Alan Connolly. The most dangerous man in Leeds."

# Chapter 2

**Friday 4 April 1975. Paris, France.**

*Home Loan Shock- Rate Rise Inevitable – A mortgage rate increase of half a per cent is almost inevitable this year, a Yorkshire building society chief said today. Mr RT Gardner, Chief Executive of the Yorkshire Association of Building Societies said an increase to 11.5% or 12% was likely due to the largest increase in building society taxation in history in 1974, and probable further increases in the forthcoming budget.*

"Garçon, another brandy. You want another drink Brendan?"

The young Irishman lifted his face from his hands and looked across the cafe table at his drinking partner.

"Yeah two more...and two more beers." The American accent was a deep booming tenor with a sandpaper edge and its cadence carried across the cobbles of Pigalle's narrow Rue Véron.

"You gotta stop crying Brendan, gotta stop living in the past."

The Irishman gazed at his own red eyed reflection in the American's mirrored shades. The eyes are the doorway to your soul, that's what his mother had said. It made sense now, because he didn't think the American had one.

"You gotta start living your life. Start smiling, like me." The American's thin lips parted briefly beneath a dark moustache speckled grey and tinted yellow beneath the nostrils. A tendril of smoke, expelled from the corner of his mouth, drifted across the table.

"I've met a lot of guys like you Brendan, and I don't like what I see." The American ran his fingers through his thinning hair, pulling the small pony tail tight at the nape of his neck.

"Fucking pussies, living in the past. Always too fucking emotional....Thanks Pierre." The American drained the glass in his hand and placed it on the waiter's tray.

"The night is young and we're gonna have some fun Brendan. We're gonna put that smile back on your face, get those Irish eyes smiling again."

The young Irishman put his face back into his hands and stared at the table.

"My name isn't Brendan. Why do you always call me that?"

The American threw back his head and laughed, scattering two pigeons which were pecking and scratching around his feet.

"Fuck it, I don't know what your fucking name is, I don't care. Come on, give me a smile." The American produced a Minolta camera from his jacket pocket and twisted the focus dial as he levelled it in the eyeline of the young man.

"Fuck off with that will you!"

The American depressed the camera shutter twice and placed the camera back in the inside pocket of his jacket, then shoved back the chair, stood and stretched.

" Come on buddy, let's go out and get you loaded, put that smile back in those eyes, that's all that matters right now."

# Chapter 3

### Saturday 5 April 1975. Leeds, England.

***Keegan Sinks United 2-0***. *Kevin Keegan punished Leeds Utd for defensive slips at Elland Road this afternoon. He grabbed goals in the $41^{st}$ and $51^{st}$ minutes as Liverpool won 2-0. Leeds who were without leading scorer Clarke, fullback Reaney and schemer Giles (all injured) are now in $10^{th}$ place, 7 points behind leaders Everton, and are facing a battle for a top 5 finish which would be needed to secure a place in next seasons' UEFA cup if they fail in their bid to win the European Cup.*

"She's already gone Alan, they wanted her at 'pub early."

The fat man with the blue and white striped apron lowered the Green Post and forced a nervous smile from behind the counter, but Alan Connolly didn't see it. He was already on his way back up the steps of the El Toro coffee bar, trying to quieten the voices in his head. Out onto Boar Lane, the old YEP seller pushing a Green Final towards him. "After today? You're joking aren't you pal?"

Dodging early Saturday night drinkers, pushing open the green wooden doors, into The Peel, trying to slow his breathing, to stop that switch in his head from being flicked. Still wired wrong. Middle aged men with beards, a group of lads back from the game, a courting couple gazing into each others' eyes across a table full of Freddie Truemans. Websters Pennine Bitter, driving out the northern thirst.

Rita behind the bar, a pink plastic mirror in one hand, an afro comb in the other, teasing her dark hair into a perfect four inch dome. *'She'll look good in that cage tonight brother.'*

"Shut the fuck up." Alan Connolly snarled to himself as Rita sensed his presence and lowered the mirror.

"Alright babe." Connolly smiled and felt his mouth turn dry and his chest tighten, as it had every single time he'd seen her in the last two years.

"Bloody hell, Alan, what are you doing? You're scratched, you'll get me sacked if Trevor sees you." She pushed herself from the barstool she'd been perched on, and the men with beards stopped talking and looked across at Alan.

"Have you seen him?" Alan motioned with his head and Rita joined him at the far end of the bar, out of earshot of the beards.

"Who? Steve? No, I rang him but he wasn't there. Julie hadn't seen him since last night."

"Fuck! So you don't know if he went and delivered the message?" Alan picked up an empty pint pot from the bar and ran his knuckles over the dimples.

"How do I know? I'm his sister not his mother, Alan."

"Fucking hell Rita, it's important!" His raised voice caused the beards to glance over again, and the voice whispered too loud in his head. *'Smash the cunts with the glass brother, go on...'*

Rita shook her head and turned away, picking up some empties and carrying them to the sink.

"Is he putting you in that cage again later?"

"What?" She turned again, her eyes flashing a mix of anger and sadness.

"Are you dancing in that fucking cage later?"

"Piss off Alan."

"Because you know why he puts you in there don't you, why it's always you and not Elaine or Tanya..." He followed her along the bar, his fingers wrapped tight around the empty pint pot and now the beards didn't look, they turned away, heads lowered.

Rita stood behind the bar, hands on hips, chewing gum that wasn't there.

"No, but I'm sure you're about to tell me Alan."

He leant across the bar, releasing the glass from his grasp.

"It's because you're black."

"I'm not black."

"You're dad's black, and to Trevor, that makes you black."

"So what's that got to do with dancing?" Rita breathed heavily through her nose and pushed out her lower lip as Alan Connolly took a step back and shrugged.

"You tell me. Maybe a slave thing. Turns him on..."

"Oh just fuck off Alan!" Her raised voice cut through the low hum of chatter in the bar and all that remained was Terry Jacks on the jukebox. *We had joy we had fun we had Man U on the run.*

Out of the Peel turning right up Albion Street, pausing to look at a pair of Prince-of-Wales checked 22' parallels in

Brills and a nice blue kipper tie in Cecil Gee. Right along Albion Place then left up Lands Lane past the empty shell of the King Charles pub, now being swallowed up by the new Schofield's store, wide concrete eyes staring down at the Victorian arcades.

Through the doors of the Three Legs into a fog of smoke and Tetley Bitter, Cossack and Hai Karate. Lads in patch-covered denim jackets and silk scarves moaning about the game, mingling with stay-at-homes in their Saturday night suits. Girls in maxi-dresses and five-inch cork soled clogs swayed to The Hustle by Van McCoy, Babycham bowl in one hand, a Consulate in the other.

Pushing through the crowd. Hands shaken, back patted, faces smiling 'Drink Alan?', 'Alright Al'.

Heads turned away. 'Do you know who he is?' 'That's Mad Alan that is.'

The lads occupying three tables in the corner, Non-stop Nigel on the one-armed bandit.

"Dennis, where's Marco got you and Nigel grafting tonight?"

Dennis Copley removed the Panatella cigar from his mouth and placed it in an ashtray on the table then straightened his two-inch-wide tie knot.

"I'm at 'Pentagon. Doors open at half nine so shift starts at nine. Nige is up at Cinderella's"

Alan Connolly nodded. "Time then. Drink up. We've got a job to do."

Dennis swilled the remainder of his pint and picked up his cigar then nudged Nigel.

"Last pull big man, we're off."

In the corner, a dark-haired teenager in flared pin-stripe trousers and a three-star jumper stood up and awkwardly negotiated the bar stools around the table.

"Can I come Alan?"

"Nah kid, I promised your old man I'd keep you out of trouble and I've not done a great job of that lately have I?" He smiled and pointed to the Tuesday night bruise now turning purple above the lad's eye.

"Nigel, Dennis, come on, we've not got all night..."

Dennis Copley stood on his toe ends and stretched his arms above the large figure hunched over the bandit, then placed his hands over Nigel's eyes. The rest of the lads cheered as Nigel turned and flailed at Dennis who made his escape towards the bar.

Alan Connolly began to button up his black leather trench coat, feeling the weight of the shotgun in the lining, trying to block out his brother's voice, to stay rational, focused, keep his emotions and Keith under control. He nodded towards the door and allowed Dennis and Nigel to pass, then turned back and caught the eye of the teenager.

"Max...okay son, you can come. Just don't tell your dad eh?"

# Chapter 4

"Same again George." Garnett Walsh drained the remainder of his rum and coke and tipped back the glass, capturing the ice cubes on his tongue before crunching them with his 9-carat teeth. George Brown nodded and swayed slowly across the bar of the Hayfield Hotel, his head nodding along to 'The Harder they Come' by Jimmy Cliff.

Garnett scowled and shook his head, trying to blank out the screeched argument of three street hookers at the end of the bar. Lopsided Afro wigs and smudged blue eye-shadow told the story of an already long day and it wasn't even 8pm. At the other side of the room a table of old men in pork-pie hats and flat caps smashed their dominoes down with a crack, and in the doorway Delroy and Marcus haggled over a deal with two long haired white boys with eyes like scared cows.

Garnett Walsh liked this time, when most of Chapeltown's night time population were still picking out their clothes for the night, making their hair big and putting on their make-up, then making phone calls, arranging where to meet. The Ffordy or Gaiety, maybe the number 8 bus into town then back to the 148 or the 'Nash or the Lamporte.

The white boys had been replaced in the doorway by a couple of street girls, driving a hard bargain, trying to cut a deal. One grabbed at Delroy's crotch and he pushed her hand away, glancing across at Garnett, eager for him to see that the approach had been rebuffed. Business was business, no room for fussing with the girls.

Wilbur was on watch, sat in the bay window. A good kid, Marcus's brother, only sixteen but brave and keen. One to watch for the future. Garnett had heard the car pull in from Chapeltown Road, the crunch of gravel, the tyres spinning as the driver negotiated the turn in third gear. He felt his heart rate quicken as he heard the low clunk of four doors opening, saw Wilbur rise slowly, his neck craning to see the occupants step out onto the car park. Garnett was off the bar stool now, as Wilbur turned, pointing out of the bay window, mouthing words lost to the sound of the tall speaker in the room corner. *The harder they come, the harder they fall, one and all.*

By the time Garnett had reached the window, Delroy and Marcus were already there and were joined by two of the arguing prostitutes.

"Who the fuck are they?" The teenage girl in the Bet Lynch wig muttered to herself but her friend answered anyway.

"That's Mad Alan from Harehills."

A K-reg Avenger. Four men, three pushing thirty, one in his late teens. Two of the older men scanned the car park, paying particularly attention to the doorway of the pub. The youngest man positioned himself at the open driver's side door. Garnett tilted his head, straining to hear the sounds from the car park above Jimmy Cliff's patois, but a slight vibration of the exhaust confirmed what he suspected-the Avenger's engine was still running.

"Marcus, go get the gun."

The dark haired man in the full length leather trench coat was approaching the pub, nodding in time to the music, a slight smile playing on his lips as he silently mouthed the lyrics. *'As sure as the sun will shine, I'm gonna get my share, what's mine.'* His eyes narrowed as he attempted to see into the dark interior of the pub and Garnett Walsh had to stop himself instinctively taking a backward step.

"What do they want?" Delroy had positioned himself alongside Garnett and the two of them watched in silence as the man in the leather coat turned away from the pub and began walking slowly across the car park. The other men maintained their position beside the Avenger, staring at the door and windows of the pub.

"Where's he going now?" Delroy's voice was almost a whisper and Garnett Walsh didn't respond, but he knew. He knew as he watched the man in the long black coat, slowly crossing the car park, glancing occasionally back towards the pub, the slight smile turning into a broad grin. He knew as the man unbuttoned his leather trench coat, knew as he removed the sawn-off shotgun from the lining and brandished it, the barrel pointing skywards. Knew as he reached the car, the red J-reg Triumph Stag that Garnett Walsh had travelled to London to buy for three grand two months earlier.

"Fucking hell..." Delroy, gripped Garnett's arm as the man circled the car, running the gun barrel along the convertible's black soft-top before taking a step back. Garnett shook himself free, stepping towards the window as the first blast caused the car's windscreen to dissolve in a thousand glass crystals. The second shot took out a front tyre and Garnett Walsh pressed his nose to the window as the screams of the prostitutes drowned out Jimmy Cliff and the man in the car park cocked the barrel of the gun to reload.

The three men standing alongside the Avenger appeared nervous, shuffling their feet and shifting their stare from the pub to the car park entrance, but the man in the trench coat seemed at ease, circling the Triumph like an inept hunter finishing off a wounded beast. Two shots, reload. Two shots, reload. By the time he began to slowly walk back across the car park, the shotgun rested casually upon the shoulder of his leather coat, the Stag had no windows and all four tyres and four headlights had been blown away. A viscous yellow liquid poured onto the gravel from the engine, which had taken two direct hits to the leaping deer emblem on the radiator grill.

"Motherfucker!" Delroy reappeared from the gents toilets, unwrapping a blue towel to reveal a rusted revolver. "Is this loaded? I can't remember..."

"Leave it." Garnett Walsh stared out towards the car park, his nose an inch from the window, and now the man in the trench coat saw him for the first time and stepped slowly forward. He cocked the shotgun and retrieved two shells from his side pocket and slid them into the barrel, then levelled the gun at waist height.

The prostitutes were now at the other side of the room next to the bar, behind which George Brown was crouched with the old dominoes players. Delroy and Marcus ducked behind the maroon velvet curtains, but Garnett Walsh remained in the bay window, his gaze fixed on the man in the trench coat who was still advancing towards the pub, shotgun extended and finger on the trigger.

"Boss, get down." Delroy breathed heavily and pressed himself against the wall beside the window.

"He won't shoot me. This is just a warning." Garnett Walsh stared out of the window at Alan Connolly, who slowly lifted the gun skywards then pulled the trigger twice, causing the prostitutes to scream and Delroy and Marcus to cover their heads and duck.

Alan Connolly smiled and nodded, then turned and slowly walked back towards the Avenger as Garnett Walsh stared at his destroyed car and whispered to no one.

"Mad Alan... there's a saying, don't get mad, get even. He gets mad, I just get even. I think it's about time I taught our friend Mr. Connolly that all actions have consequences, and they can be a lot more serious than a written-off motor."

# Chapter 5

**Sunday 6 April 1975. Paris.**

*Thatcher Snubs Enoch – Tory leadership challenger Margaret Thatcher has given the thumbs-down to rebel Enoch Powell. She is firmly opposed to allowing him back into the Tory fold. Mrs. Thatcher has branded him a traitor – a man who abandoned his supporters and twice voted Labour.*

"Where'd you have your hair cut Brendan?" The American spluttered a half-cough as he exhaled, and a thin veil of smoke drifted across the cafe table and prickled Jimmy Dolan's eyes.

"What? My hair?"

"Yeah your fucking hair man. Did someone steal it?"

"Steal my hair? I don't understand..." the young Irishman rubbed at his temples. "My fucking head hurts. What time did I go back to the room last night?"

"Who cares. Lighten up." The American tipped back his head and poured the contents of a spirit glass into his mouth and crunched on an ice cube.

"Jesus, I think I'm going to puke." Jimmy Dolan leant back and stared up at a Paris sky the colour of drowned flesh.

"Yeah well...I think someone stole your hair. Or your toe nails. Always flush your toe nails and your finger nails Brendan. Someone gets hold of that shit, they pretty much own you."

"What? My toe nails. Jesus, I don't know what the fuck you're talking about."

"You can laugh, but I've seen that shit go down. In Haiti. Fucking hair and toe nails...the houngan, the voodoo witch doctor guy...he can use that shit for a spell. A hex, like a fucking curse Brendan. That's what happened to you. Someone cursed you man. That's why you can't snap out of this fucking mood. So fucking...morose, man!

"Pierre... water, s'il vous plait." Jimmy Dolan raised a finger to attract the waiter's attention.

"What's that, water? No fucking way man. No wonder you feel ill, these fuckers serve tap water, half a pint of rat piss and shit. Get him a beer Pierre. And a brandy."

"Oh for fucks sake. No. I need to sleep."

"You can sleep forever when you're dead Brendan. For now you're spending time in Paris, France with Simeon Crook III, and we have more important things to do than sleep, my friend. Pierre, fix this man a proper drink and let the new day begin!"

# Chapter 6

**Sunday 6 April 1975. Leeds.**

"I'm not leaving my fucking house Steve!"

"I'm just saying...it might be safer, just for a bit, till all this dies down."

"And where would I go?" Rita Bernard turned away from her brother and extinguished a gas ring as the whistling kettle drowned out Paul Burnett on Radio 1.

"I dunno. Maybe stay at Marie's?" Steve Bernard tipped back his head to drain a coffee mug then held it out towards his sister.

"How would I get to work from there? This is my house Steve...why should I leave? It's nothing to do with me..."

"What's not?" Rita turned away and ran the coffee mug under the tap and Steve began picking at his finger nail as the hall door opened with a creak, and Alan Connolly entered the kitchen, barechested.

"I said what's got nothing to do with you?" Alan sat down at the table opposite Steve who remained silent and flicked at a splash of mud on his new Onitsuka basketball boots.

Rita muttered unintelligible words from the sink and Steve took a deep breath before speaking.

"This shit with Walsh."

"You heard about his motor then?" Alan smiled and rubbed at the stubble on his chin. "Get us a coffee Reets."

"I think everyone in North Leeds heard about his motor Alan..." Steve sniffed and shook his head.

"What's your fucking problem?"

Steve Bernard carried on looking at the floor under the weight of Alan's stare, as Cockney Rebel crackled an invitation from the radio to come up and see them, make them smile.

"What was I meant to do? He's taking the fucking piss the fat wee cunt."

"Shooters though Alan..." Steve shook his head.

"I had to do something to get his attention. He's been taking the piss."

"Yeah well...two sugars please sis...I'm pretty sure you got his attention. What happens now?"

Alan Connolly stood and removed a bag of sugar from the kitchen cupboard.

"What happens now is that he stops fucking selling his stuff on our patch. He stays on his side of Roundhay Road."

"Strega's on his side of..."

"Fuck off Steve, the Strega is different, it's Harehills, its ours. That was agreed two years back. Gaiety is his, Strega's ours. It's not just the Strega, they've been selling in Hernie's."

"Apparently."

"What's that mean? They were in there. To be honest, I don't fucking care whether they were selling or not, I don't want them in our pubs and clubs. Room at the Top too, we agreed that was ours, but I know for a fact his lads have been selling stuff in there."

Rita slammed two mugs down on the kitchen table.

"So I have to move out because this Walsh kid might come and shoot me, is that right Alan?"

"Will he fuck! Steve, what are you telling her that for? He knows he was in the wrong and he's had his warning. End of story." Alan Connolly blew across the rim of the steaming mug then raised it slowly towards his lips.

"And if he comes, we'll be ready for him. Don't you worry about that Rita love."

# Chapter 7

"So what are you hearing?" Alan Connolly leant with his hands on the backyard wall of the terraced house in Lascelles Terrace.

"Well he's not fucking happy." Steve sat on the house steps clutching his coffee mug.

"Good. That was the idea. To make sure he got the message...no more selling on our side of the road."

Steve nodded. "You know why it's been happening though?"

"The International thing?"

"Yeah, since the 'Nash lost their late licence all the business is down here. His boys are left holding a load of gear they can't shift."

"That's fucking bollocks Steve. There's still plenty of business at the Hayfield, 96 Club, Lamporte, 148, Jooves, Cliff's...it's an excuse. He's taking the piss, like he has been ever since I got out."

Steve puffed out his cheeks as he exhaled loudly. "Nearly three years Alan. The deal we made has kept things pretty quiet. You just need to calm down a bit. Everyone does."

Alan Connolly pushed himself away from the wall and raised his hands in a prayer stance. "I'm calm pal. Cool. Like fucking Hare Krishna here, don't you worry about me."

# Chapter 8

### Tuesday 8 April 1975. Paris.

*6 out of 10 for Europe – Six out of ten British voters now say they will vote 'yes' in the June referendum on the common market. This is twice as many as the 28 per cent who say they will vote for Britain to pull out of Europe. The evidence of the survey suggests that public opinion has turned towards the EEC since last month's final round of negotiations in Dublin and the Labour government's recommendation to accept the new terms.*

Jimmy Dolan closed his eyes at the sound of a loud double-knock on the door of his attic bedsit. He thought he'd been awake since first light but the ancient clock on the wall now said eleven.

Two more knocks in quick succession caused him to pull the soiled pillow over his head.

"Brendan, are you in there Buddy?"

"Fucking go away. Please..." his whispered words were lost to the unsilenced exhaust of a motorbike passing along Rue Jean-Baptiste.

"C'mon Brendan, open the door son. Watcha doing in there, jerkin' off?"

The door handle rattled and Jimmy Dolan threw the pillow across the room and sat up slowly, then pulled the sheets back and limped barefoot to the door. He slid back the bolt and was back in bed before the door opened and Simeon Crook III pushed his way in, wearing a wide-lapelled checked jacket and a baseball cap. In his right hand was a foot-long baguette. In his left was a half bottle of supermarket red wine.

Simeon Crook sat on the end of the bed as Jimmy Dolan pulled the blankets over his head and turned away to face the wall.

"What's eating at you buddy? Where'd you disappear to yesterday? I was worried..." Jimmy flinched at the touch of Crook's hand on his leg.

"I wasn't in the mood, that's all. Needed some time alone."

"You know what I think Brendan...?" Simeon Crook stood and walked to the small window. He tugged back the purple bath towel which served as a curtain, and a shaft of sunlight caused Dolan to blink and close one eye.

"I said, you know what I think Brendan?" The older man turned and strode back across the room, then grasped the blankets in both hands and hauled them off the bed, leaving Jimmy Dolan curled in a shivering ball, his skin waxy and grey in stark contrast to his red underpants.

"Just fuck off Crook, leave me be!"

"What I think is that you're depressed. And when you're depressed, spending time alone is not what the doctor ordered. In fact, it's the worst possible thing you can do. Here, have a drink..." Simeon Crook momentarily extended the wine bottle towards the bed, then took a large swig himself.

"You don't understand." Jimmy Dolan lifted himself from the bed and shivered, then picked up a brown leather jacket from the back of a chair, put it on and sat down at a small formica table.

"So tell me. Help me understand...why you're so fucking depressed man!" Simeon Crook took another swig from the bottle and slid it across the table as he sat down.

Dolan picked up the bottle and tilted it, watching the dark line of liquid shifting back and forth.

"I've done a bad thing." He sighed and shook his head and lifted the bottle to his mouth, tipping it back and swallowing hard.

"We've all done bad things Brendan."

"Yeah but, the thing I did was..." Jimmy Dolan shook his head and brought his hands up to cover his face.

"Very bad?" Simeon Crook III extended his hand and took back the bottle, a smile playing on his lips.

Jimmy Dolan nodded. "The worst."

"Interesting." Simeon Crook took a large swig of wine then ripped off the end of the baguette and chewed it noisily.

"If I tell you..."

"You know what they say Brendan. A trouble shared and all that..." Breadcrumbs spilled onto Crook's chin as he spoke and chewed.

Jimmy Dolan nodded, inhaled deeply through his nostrils and stared at the cracked ceiling of the bedsit.

"I murdered someone."

Jimmy Dolan closed his eyes, his head still tilted upwards. It felt good to have finally said it and he could hear his breathing begin to slow, with only the ticking of the clock disturbing the silence in the room.

He heard the wine bottle being lifted from the table and slowly lowered his head and opened his eyes to see the tanned, lined face of Simeon Crook grinning back at him, crumbs speckling his grey moustache.

"Is that it? We've all fucking murdered someone Brendan."

"No...not like this."

Crook smirked as he lifted the wine bottle to his lips, then replaced it on the table without drinking, and reached into his pocket for a packet of Gauloises. Jimmy Dolan fought to suppress his anger at the casual acceptance of the sin he'd committed.

"So who did you kill then? Go on, tell me..." Crook flicked at his lighter and his cigarette glowed orange as he inhaled.

Dolan stood up and walked to the door. He turned the handle and peered round the door frame into the stairwell, then stepped back into the room and locked the door, facing Simeon Crook in his leather jacket and red underpants. He walked to the window and looked out, then drew the purple bath towel to block out the light. Now he couldn't see the older man's features, only the glow of his cigarette in the centre of the room.

"I'm Irish right...Catholic, from Newry. Bandit country they call it. Half and half. I got in a bit of trouble when I was a kid, just nicking cars and stuff. Ended up in an approved school. Borstal. The idea is they toughen you up, teach you a skill so you can get work when you get out." The words poured out like a rapid exhalation after a suppressed breath.

"Yeah, we call it Juvie in the states..."

"Shut up and listen. You wanted to know, now I'm telling you." Jimmy Dolan's snapped response caused Crook to raise his hands in mock surrender.

"So I learnt a few things in there. Mainly how to nick better cars and not get caught. I also got mates with a few lads who were connected, with the 'Ra you know? They always liked to use kids from the schools as they knew we could fly under the radar, and if we got caught it was a slap on the wrist rather than jail time. Good money though for a kid of 16,17. I started doing jobs, mainly driving for the guys collecting protection money, you know?"

Simeon Crook narrowed his eyes as he drew on his cigarette, his head tilted slightly.

"Anyway, it was just after Christmas and I was totally fucking skint. I was seeing this girl and we'd been living it up a bit. Out every night, buying decent gear, records, you know the story. My pal told me they were looking for someone to do a job. Drive a van over to England, drop it off with a lassie called Judy in Derby, then get the train up to Liverpool and the ferry home. Three hundred quid for the job, easy, I told them I wanted to do it."

"When was this?" Simeon Crook turned his cigarette between two fingers and thumb, examining the glowing ash as if noticing it for the first time.

"January last year. Anyway, I picked the van up, it was full of sealed crates, marked up as some sort of engineering parts. I didn't ask, didn't want to know. They'd booked me on the ferry from Larne to Stranraer, it was snowing like fuck when I picked it up..."

"I know what you did." Simeon Crook drew on the cigarette, and it glowed in the half-light, illuminating his features in an orange glow. He wasn't smirking anymore.

"What? You know..."

"It's fucking obvious Brendan. February 4$^{th}$ 1974. My-oh-my buddy, you have been a bad boy haven't you? No wonder you're feeling so blue."

# Chapter 9

**Tuesday, 8 April 1975, Leeds.**

Alan Connolly had first spotted the brown Vauxhall Viva parked with the engine running outside St. Aiden's church, so he'd crossed the road by the Kosher Butcher's and turned down Whitfield Street past the Cabana Club, then along the ginnels to Gathorne Street. Now there it was again. Parked on Gipton Avenue, brake lights red and two shadows in the front seats. *Told you to get a lift brother. Not safe for you round here anymore.*

He kept walking and was still looking over his shoulder when he reached the lock-up garage which housed 'Sir Norms' records.

"Alright Al?" Norman Cowell was straightening the LPs in a wooden crate in front of the blue shuttered doors.

"I'm alright Norm, how's things with you and your girl?"

"Good. Two years now. We're even talking about getting one of those Vietnamese babies."

"Fuck me. Business booming then?" Alan picked the frayed sleeve of 'Can't Get Enough' by Barry White from one of the crates. "Branching out from Rocksteady are you?"

"One for 'mums that one mate! Not so much Rocksteady now though, 'kids are getting into this Dub Reggae, King Tubby and Lee Scratch Perry, stuff like that."

Alan Connolly smiled. "What happened to that kid in the parka from ten years back? You'll be growing an afro next!"

"You've got to move with 'times in this business. Not still listening to the Stones are you? I could just about stand 'Goat's Head Soup' but that last album was fucking shite!"

"I'm worried about you Norman. You still don't understand good music, I think you're in the wrong business son... Got any Roxy Music? I quite like them. That kid who sings looks cool as fuck."

"They're not right popular in Chappie I'm afraid." Norman laughed. "I'm doing a bit of DJ'ing too. Cats Whiskers in Meanwood. They do Northern Soul all-dayers on Bank Holidays. Kids there from all over 'country."

Alan Connolly raised his eyebrows. "Who's doing the speed?"

Norman shook his head. "Local firm backed by 'Hyde Park lads out of 'Newlands. Don't even consider it. Anyway, you sorted me out for the match then?"

Alan Connolly reached into the breast pocket of his leather trench coat and handed over two folded slips of paper, glancing over Norman's shoulder at the brown car appearing from Spencer Mount and pausing, before carrying on towards Gathorne Terrace.

"Cheers mate, I was struggling there." Norman unfolded the tickets and grinned as he displayed them, one in each hand. "Same ticket numbers!"

"What did you expect? You'll be alright, just don't go through the turnstile together." Alan maintained his focus over Norman's shoulder.

"How many have you got?"

"Inky Tony ran us a couple of hundred off. I didn't want too many. Flooding the market just pushes the price down. Max and a few of the young lads are taking the day off tomorrow to flog them in town and outside the ground. Should get £6 for a quid standing ticket I reckon."

Norman nodded. "Business alright again now then?"

Alan shifted his gaze back to his friend and interpreted the deeper meaning in the question.

"What are you hearing on this side of the road?"

Norman looked left and right and stepped inside the shop, a nod of the head telling Alan to follow him.

"Walsh is fucked right off Alan." Norman drummed his fingers on a pile of 45's on either side of the narrow aisle down the centre of the lock-up. "You made him look a right cunt. His car was stuck outside 'Hayfield for two days, rubbing his nose in it. His lads can't understand why he hasn't done owt about it."

"Two reasons Norm – one, he's been taking the piss and he knows it. Two, he knows that whatever he does to me, he'll get back, twice as hard."

"Just be careful mate, that's all I'm saying. He's a sneaky bastard and I've a feeling he's planning something."

"Like what?" A car passed slowly along the road outside and Alan felt the familiar pulse of electricity as his heart pumped harder. *Calm down brother, it's a red Toyota.*

"Like he has his ear to the ground. He knows stuff. And word on the street has always been that he's prepared to talk to the law when he needs a favour."

"So what? What's he know?"

"Stuff that you don't want anyone talking about Al."

Alan Connolly nodded and the shotgun in the lining of his trench coat suddenly felt heavier.

"See you in town before the game tomorrow. We'll be in the Legs from dinnertime if you fancy it?"

"Wednesday. Half day closing. I'll see you there. We can talk about how we're getting to Paris for 'final!"

# Chapter 10

### Wednesday, 9 April 1975, Leeds.

*Cup Touts Get the Wind up! Visitors to Elland Road today ran the gauntlet of a dozen touts selling tickets for tonight's European cup match between Leeds and Barcelona. But customers were few and far between and it turned into a cold wait in the strong wind for most of the touts. Today's handful of early customers were naming their own price, although £1 ground tickets were said to be going for about £5 or £6, but touts were confident of getting £20 for £4 stand tickets by kick off. A small party of Barcelona supporters, mostly middle aged businessmen and their wives, came with the team on the flight from Spain and have been staying at the Dragonara Hotel.*

"Yorkshire Television are fucking traitors Alan, I tell you! If Leeds lose tonight we should get all 'lads down to Kirkstall Road to have a serious word." Max Jackson swayed on the packed terrace of Elland Road's new South Stand.

"What, so they let Rinus Michels watch all this season's games on video tape?" Dennis Copley shoved his head between them from the terrace step above.

"Not just Michels. Cruyff, Neeskens, the whole team. Gave them a private screening last night. I read it in 'Evening Post. The cheeky bastards!"

"So you've been sat reading the paper in the cafe half the afternoon rather than shifting tickets. No wonder you ended up knocking them out for a couple of quid." Alan

Connolly stared out towards the floodlit pitch through a drifting haze of cigarette smoke.

"It was fucking freezing Alan. We had to take it in turns to go get warmed up. There was always one of us out selling though, honest."

"Barely broke even. You're lucky. If I'd lost money you'd have been paying it back from your pocket money son."

Max's mumbled apology was lost in a crescendo of boos and whistles as Johan Cruyff led the Barcelona team from the tunnel.

"Good move from Armfield leaving Norman out." Dennis Copley was captain of the Fforde Grene Red Triangle league side and saw himself as the tactical expert of the LS9 Asylum. "Madeley's got more pace. We'll need that against Cruyff and Asensi."

"Lorimer on the bench though and Yorath in. What's the point of that?" Max Jackson's question went unanswered as Bremner led the Leeds team onto the pitch to be greeted by a deafening rendition of 'We're gonna win the European Cup'. Max's young gang stuck with the more familiar version of the tune and 'You're gonna get your fucking heads kicked in' as they jabbed fingers towards the fifty or so suit-wearing Barcelona fans seated in the West Stand.

The game kicked off with Leeds dictating the pace, obviously eager to prevent Barcelona playing their passing game, but the Spaniards showed they weren't afraid of a battle, as Marinho Peres steamed into an early challenge on Jordan, causing the South Stand crowd to surge forward.

"Fucking dirty Spanish bastard!" spat Max's mate Geoff.

"He's Brazilian son." Alan Connolly hauled the kid back into place on the step in front of him.

Five minutes later they were roaring again as Clarke chased a through ball from Bremner and left his boot in the face of Barca keeper Sadurni.

The tension on the packed terrace was increased by the number of fans who'd spent an afternoon drinking around town and, unable to fight their way down to the concourse toilets, went where they stood.

"Fuck's sake I'm stood in piss here. Was that you ya dirty bastard?" Alan turned and glared into the face of a swaying man in a tartan cap two terrace steps back, as Giles floated a long ball forward towards Jordan.

The man looked up and was about to reply as the big striker nodded the ball down to Bremner, advancing into the penalty area at speed, with no defenders in sight. The Leeds captain hit his shot perfectly and the man in the tartan cap froze, mouth open, as the ball flew into the top corner of the net, directly in front of the South Stand terrace. The stand erupted in a mass surge of celebrating bodies. Ten minutes gone and Leeds had the perfect start and the weight of tension in the ground lifted instantly.

Barcelona were rocking now and McQueen went close with a trademark header, then Eddie Gray went past De la Cruz like he wasn't there, and a chip from his brother Frank missed by inches. Salvador Sadurni in the Barcelona goal was clearly unsettled and flapped at crosses as Leeds won four corners in a minute in front of the South Stand but the Spaniards held out and were clearly relieved to hear the half time whistle.

"Let them off the hook there. I hope we don't live to regret that." Alan Connolly turned to see Norman pushing his way through the crowd to squeeze onto the terrace beside him.

"You got in alright then?"

"Yeah no bother. How did ticket sales go?"

"Pretty shit to be honest, I think Max and his mates spent most of the afternoon chatting the birds in the café up. Ended up knocking them out at two quid before kick off."

"I told you Alan, there was no one buying. Not at the prices we were asking anyway." Max caught Norman's eye and winked.

The second half kicked off with a scrap between Yorath and half the Barcelona team following a foul on Gray, prompting 'Gelderd Aggro' to ring out from eight thousand voices on the Kop.

After 65 minutes a Leeds attack broke down and Cruyff brought the ball out of defence and fed Heredia who bore down on the Leeds goal with Reaney hot on his heels.

"Yes! What a fucking tackle! Dennis Copley punched the air as the Leeds fullback deftly nicked the ball from beneath the feet of the Barcelona striker. "What?? He's given a free kick. The ref was miles away, he couldn't see that."

"Cheating bastards! Only a foot outside 'area too. Cruyff will have a go at this. I can't watch." Norman put his hands over his eyes as Barcelona's star player stood over the ball with Rexach alongside him. Leeds had all eleven players in their own penalty area, and were still trying to arrange their defensive wall as Cruyff rolled the ball to his left and Juan Manuel Asensi calmly side footed it into the corner of the Leeds net.

"Bastard!" Max sent a half full cup of Bovril arcing towards the pitch as boos rang out from around the ground and the Barcelona supporters in the West Stand stood and applauded politely.

The noise from the crowd was a constant, deafening crescendo rolling down the terraces and echoing across the pitch, and with Leeds attacking the Kop in waves, it almost felt like they were playing downhill.

"Barcelona are hanging on here. We need another goal. Going over there with a draw won't be enough." Norman spoke almost to himself as Madeley strode out of defence with the ball and Alan was shoved forward by a crowd surge from behind.

Madeley fed Reaney on the right wing and Alan felt hands on his shoulders pull him back into position as a head appeared over his left shoulder.

"Alright Al." He turned to see Chris, a kid from Cross Gates who worked with Inky Tony.

"Alright son." Alan turned back to face the pitch as Reaney knocked the ball past a Barcelona defender and floated a cross towards Jordan in the penalty area.

"Have you heard?" Chris shouted into Alan's ear as Jordan connected with the ball and knocked it down towards Yorath.

"No, heard what?"

Yorath missed the ball and it bounced loose on the edge of the six yard box where Clarke was lurking, to hit it perfectly on the half volley.

The South Stand terrace was already bouncing in celebration before the ball hit the net and Alan found himself propelled forward, being hugged by Norman and Max, to end up fifteen feet down the terrace.

"Fucking yes! That will do it. Paris here we come!" Dennis Copley was trying to haul himself up onto a crash barrier as the whole ground began to chant 'We're gonna win the European Cup!'

"Ten minutes left. Time for another one yet. Make sure of it." Norman turned back and grinned at Alan who smelt old beer and sensed Chris breathing into his ear from the step behind.

"So you've not heard Al?"

"Not heard what?" Alan twisted on the terrace step to turn his head towards the swaying youth with collar length hair in a centre parting.

"About Tony....Inky."

"What about him?"

"Got nicked today. Coppers raided 'unit."

"What?...Why?" Alan now turned his back to the pitch and faced Chris.

"Not sure, but 'only thing we've done off 'books lately is them tickets for you, so I'm guessing it must be that."

"Fucking hell. What did the law say?"

"Said they were acting on information received. Sounds like someone's grassed. Not good that is it?"

"You're right son, it's not good. Not good at all. Especially if the grass is who I think it might be."

# Chapter 11

**Friday 11 April 1975, Paris.**

*Prices up Record 4p in the Pound- Prices took a record leap last month – a savage rise of nearly 4p in the pound, it was revealed today. The annual rate of inflation is now running at a record level of 24% and is rapidly catching up with average earnings which are running at 29%. The figures show that if price rises in the last 12 months are taken together, the last three months show a terrifying upward jump of more than a third.*

"I don't really feel bad about the soldiers, even though most of them were just young boys. It's the two wee kiddies that I can't get out of my head. Five and two, and their ma. They didn't deserve that just because their dad was a squaddie."

"Collateral damage Brendan. It's the same in any war. Just the way it has to be."

Simeon Crook III reached into the basket on the café table and picked up a baguette, which he tore into quarters then tossed towards a pigeon pecking at the pavement of Place St Georges.

"And that poor little lad, six years old, burnt from head to toe, still in hospital last time..." Jimmy Dolan stared into his empty glass and shook his head.

"Ok buddy, we get the picture! You thought you were blowing up a bus full of soldiers but it turned out their families were on there too. Big fucking surprise! Jeez

Brendan, you sure know how to bring the mood down son."

"I didn't know though...that's the point. I was just delivering a van. I didn't know what was in it..."

"That's a crock of BS Brendan and you know it! In the name of God son, what did you think was in the fucking van? Engine parts? BULL-SHIT! And you know it. Own your fucking actions man. Live with it."

The two men fell silent as a waiter brushed crumbs from the table and cleared empty glasses.

"Encore monsieur?

"Yeah, fill em up Pierre." Simeon Crook lit a cigarette and stared hard at Jimmy Dolan who blinked back tears and stared at his feet.

"So why Paris?" Crook drew on the Gauloises and blew smoke across the table into Dolan's face.

"What do you mean?"

"Why are you here, in Paris, a year on? What's the plan?"

"I don't know. They just told me I had to get out when the girl, Judith, got picked up. I was eating my tea with my mam and da' and my little brother and there was a knock at the door. Two fellas I'd never seen before. They told me to pack a bag, that Special Branch knew my name and I had to leave right then. Pulled a gun on me when I tried to argue. I never even got time to say goodbye to Helen...she was my girlfriend. They said if I tried to contact her they'd have to kill her."

"You were lucky." Simeon Crook tossed another lump of bread to the pigeon.

"Lucky? How the fuck am I lucky? My fucking life is over. I'm stuck here, can't contact anyone, can't work, I'm just living off the bit of cash they drop me every month."

"You're lucky because if you worked for my old company you'd be dead. You're a loose end. An inconvenience. They've got what they wanted from you , you're no further use to them. I'm just surprised they've kept you alive."

"Well, my uncle had connections in the 'Ra military council. Maybe he had a word, I don't know."

"How did you get here? Did you have a passport?"

"Didn't have one. I'd never been abroad before. Because it all happened so fast they didn't have time to get their usual guy to make one, so they gave me one with a photo of someone ten years older than me, looks nothing like me. They got me across the border and I got a ferry from Cork where the 'Ra have someone on customs. Landed at Roscoff at 4am when the frogs were half asleep and they just waved me through. I'd never get back with it though so I'm stuck here. Thinking about what I did all day, every day. And you say I'm lucky?"

"You're alive buddy. You're in a beautiful city. It's springtime, and you know what's your biggest stroke of luck of all?"

"Tell me." Jimmy Dolan flicked his foot out and the pigeon clucked and fluttered its wings and he watched it take off half heartedly then land again ten feet away.

"Your biggest stroke of luck Brendan was meeting Simeon Crook III. Don't worry son, I'm going to pull you out of this depression. Things are going to get better, believe me."

# Chapter 12

**Sunday 13 April 1975, Leeds.**

*Fan Ban- London Tube train staff are threatening a 24 hour walk out in a protest against football hooliganism. They aim to stop services on May 24 -the date of the next England-Scotland match at Wembley. Mr Bob Kettle, of the NUR executive said 'the last game was the final straw. 'The fans just went berserk at Wembley station, urinating all over the place and running over the track.'*

"You got rid of it then?" Alan Connolly looked up from the Sunday People as Steve Bernard entered the Grill and Griddle café on the corner of Harehills Road.

"Yeah, it's buried. And the ammo. Owt else you need me to get rid of?"

Alan Connolly puffed out his cheeks and stared down at a cold full English, the tomato running into the egg into the beans, making him feel even more sick.

"Can't think of anything mate. There's my old man's bayonet but I'm not giving that up. I need something in case that cunt Walsh turns up at the house." *Our family heir loom brother. Only thing the old bastard left us.*

"You think it was definitely him then, that got Tony lifted?"

"Only Tony and the lads who work for him know he ran us those tickets off, and they aren't going to say anything. And Norman's heard Walsh has been asking questions."

"About what?"

"About my business. Where and what I sell. I keep expecting him to make a move. Hit the supply or do some of our lads over. Fucking grassing though, that's a different level. I can't believe even he'd do that." Alan Connolly wrinkled his nose in disgust and shook his head.

"There's always been rumours about him. Never seems to get lifted, always one step ahead of 'law. I've heard that Triumph of his was always parked round 'back of the Nags at Chapel Allerton too. He never drank in there though, always 'Regent."

"Coppers pub."

"Exactly. Why else would he be drinking round there?"

Alan Connolly took a swig from a coffee mug as Steve pulled a chair up to the table.

"Well, one thing's for sure Stevie, he won't be parking that fucking Stag round there again any time soon."

Steve forced a half smile. "What was 'other thing you wanted to see me about?"

Alan looked beyond Steve, out of the café window and up Roundhay Road, monitoring the progress of a brown car as it hesitated before flicking on its indicator and turning left up Harehills Road.

"What?"

"You said on 'phone there was something you wanted me to do?"

"Was there...? Oh yeah, Whitsun Bank Holiday, end of this month. Normal was telling me the Cats Whiskers have got The Wailers and Jimmy Cliff on."

"Yeah I heard that. It's that Tubby Stan Reggae Club that are running it. They got Keen Boothe and Toots and the Maytals a couple of years back. Think you were still inside then."

"I'd just got out but I wasn't back in business. Anyway, I was thinking, we're due a delivery of Red Leb from the bloke in Hull the week before that. Those Rastafarians are into the Wailers aren't they? Reckon we could shift a load there."

Steve bit his lip and sat back in his seat. "Yeah but..."

"I know, I know. Hyde Park lads control the supply, but they just sell poor quality grass to students. They know them hardcore Rasta brothers won't go for that."

"So what are you thinking?"

"Take a sample to Kenny at the Newlands. We make good margin on it, so can afford to cut them in at 10% if they want our boys to do the selling. If they want the Meanwood lads to do it I'll give them 20% discount on the weight, but tell them your lot are more likely to buy off us."

"My lot?" Steve laughed out loud.

"You know what I mean. And it's true!" Alan Connolly drained his coffee mug and stood up, eyes scanning the door and the traffic on Roundhay Road.

"Go see him tonight. Makes sense for all of us. He'll snap our hands off. What's he got to lose?"

# Chapter 13

**Wednesday 16 April 1975, Paris.**

*Figures released today reveal that 12,000 vehicles were taken without authority in the West Yorkshire police area last year and only 4500 were recovered. Police say that precautions drivers can take against losing their vehicle include not leaving the keys in the ignition even for a short time, locking doors and securing windows, locking the boot, never leaving valuables on view and never leaving luggage on the roof.*

Jimmy Dolan blew a chunk of snot-slick carrot from his nose then slowly opened his eyes and stared at his puke spattered shoes. His throat burned and his mouth tasted of metal when he ran his dry tongue over his cracked lips.

He hauled himself painfully upright and looked around. He was sitting on a low wall in a dead-end cobbled street filled with dustbins and a rusting Renault 4L with deflated tyres. A stinging sensation in his groin told him he'd probably pissed himself a couple of hours earlier.

He stood up and spotted a pair of legs splayed in a V-shape on the cobbles between two over-flowing bins. There was no shoe on the right foot but on the left, he recognised the tan, square-heeled cowboy boot of Simeon Crook III.

Moving towards Crook's lifeless body, Jimmy Dolan became aware that the sight in his right eye was blurred and raised his hand, then retracted it when he felt a stab of pain as he touched his eyelid. Congealed brown blood coated his fingers and he realised he was unable to fully open his eye. Further investigation revealed dried blood coating his cheek, neck and the collar of his shirt. The knee of his trousers was torn open to reveal a deep gash on his knee-cap.

"Crook...Crook..." Jimmy Dolan's first attempts at speaking resulted only in a rasping whisper, until he growled and hawked up a thick tumour of bloody phlegm from deep within his throat.

"Crook. Are you alive?"

The American was face down on the cobbles, his arms bunched up under his body. Looking down caused Dolan's vision to blur and spin, so he rested a shoe on Crook's shoulder and slowly rocked him back and forth while staring at a tattered poster on the brickwork for a Deep Purple concert.

Dolan had no idea how long he'd been prodding the lifeless body when he heard a low moan and felt the shape at his feet begin to move.

"Brendan...is that you?"

Dolan looked down into the bloodied face of Simeon Crook, his eyes blackened and closed and his nose knocked sideways and split along the bridge by a two inch gash.

"Brendan...fucking hell son. We survived!" The American began to laugh, then paused to slowly raise a hand to his mouth. He licked at his gums, then, with thumb and two fingers reached into his mouth and snapped out two front teeth.

"What a fucking night...or day. What time is it?" Simeon Crook, tilted the teeth in his fingers an inch from his nose and screwed up his eyes as he examined them, then tossed them onto the cobbles.

Jimmy Dolan tried to control the shaking in his right hand as he lifted it to pull back his jacket sleeve.

"Don't know. I've lost my watch."

Jimmy Dolan slowly lowered himself into a crouch then tumbled backwards to lie alongside Crook.

"Jesus Christ. What happened to us?"

Simeon Crook reached out and ruffled the young Irishman's hair, and began to laugh and cough.

"More to the point." Dolan looked hard into Crook's eyes. "Who are you? And what the fucking hell are you?"

# Chapter 14

**Friday 19 April 1975, Leeds.**

*Police warning in vice row- Police today appealed to angry residents not to take the law into their own hands in dealing with kerb crawlers and prostitutes in Chapeltown, Leeds. Their appeal follows a meeting of residents at which suggestions were put forward on how to curb vice on the suburb's streets. A Leeds police spokesman said 'we are well aware of the problem of street prostitution in Chapeltown, but we do advise people who are approached not to try and take the law into their own hands but to inform the police.'*

"Are you not going tomorrow then Alan?" Dennis Copley leant on the bar of the Waterloo pub, his fingers cradling a dimpled pint pot of Double Diamond.

"Nah, fucking Ipswich. Set of carrot-crunchers. Waste of time, they won't bring any boys."

"Bet he leaves a few out before Barcelona on Wednesday too." Terry Jackson lit a cigarette at the other side of the bar, then emptied a drip tray into a metal bucket and removed a slice of lemon from an empty glass on the bar and placed it in a jar filled with identical lemon slices next to the till.

"Know anyone who's going to Spain Dennis?" Norman Cowley sat on a bar stool, thumbing through a 'Scene and Heard' bag of 45's.

"Two lads from our street, Dermot and Joey are going with their uncle." Max Jackson returned to the bar with a handful of glasses.

"Everyone's saving it for Paris. Have you sorted a minibus yet Al?"

"Fucking hell Norm, you're tempting fate pal, we're not there yet. If we do get to the final though I'm thinking something a bit bigger. Maybe a 30 or 42 seater..."

"Yes! Forty Asylum lads taking over Paris, I can't wait!" Max punched the air and his father shook his head.

"How you planning to pay for that then son?" Terry Jackson picked up a handful of glasses from the bar.

"Been saving up."

"Yeah, skimming off on my Barcelona tickets no doubt, ya wee cunt!" Alan Connolly cuffed the teenager's head as he passed. The pub door opened and Steve entered and caught Alan's eye, then stepped back out through the door.

"Same again Terry." Connolly threw back the remainder of his drink and slammed his empty glass on the bar then headed towards the door.

Steve was standing on the street corner, both hands in the pockets of his leather jacket, scanning the street left and right.

"Did you see him?"

"Yeah, just been over now." Steve licked at his lips and shuffled his feet, avoiding eye contact.

"And?"

"Not interested?"

"You fucking what? Did you offer the 20%?"

"Course I did, gave him the sample too, or tried to. He wouldn't touch it."

Alan Connolly opened his mouth but didn't speak. *Something's not right here brother. Something stinks.*

Steve paced outside the pub door, hands in his pockets, facing away from Alan.

"So what did he say?"

Steve turned to face him and took a deep breath. "To be honest Alan, he didn't say much. As soon as I walked in 'Newlands his face dropped. Got off his bar stool and met me before I'd got halfway across the room, couldn't get me out of there quick enough."

"What the fuck? What's his problem?" *I think you know what the problem is brother. Who the problem is.*

"He was shit scared Alan. Asked me if I was sure I wasn't being followed and kept looking up and down 'road while he was talking to me. Told me to fuck off and not try to contact him or any of his boys again."

Alan heard his breath quicken and felt his heart beating hard in his chest. *They know brother. They can see what's coming. The writing's on the wall.*

"That's not all." Steve took his hands out of his pockets and stepped forward, rubbing his palms on his jeans. "As I was walking to the car, he shouted out to me from the pub door."

"Go on..." Alan's mouth was dry, his words came out as a whisper.

"He said, 'be careful Steve. Be careful because Alan is going down, hard, and you don't want to be anywhere near him when that happens."

# Chapter 15

**Sunday 21 April 1975, Paris.**

*Battle of White Hart Lane- Soccer's terrace animals struck long before the start of the Spurs-Chelsea relegation battle. Referee Jack Taylor, a giant butcher from Wolverhampton, helped police clear the pitch of hundreds of fighting supporters. Spurs goalkeeper Pat Jennings was attacked by two louts as he ran onto the pitch, while back on the terraces a police officer was battered to the ground and others were forced to draw truncheons to extract him from a dangerous situation.*

"So why are we here?" Jimmy Dolan picked at the scab above his right eye and stared up at the twin towers of Notre Dame cathedral from a bench in the shadow of a statue of Charlemagne.

Alongside him, Simeon Crook III squinted through swollen eyelids and sucked hard on a Gauloises through his scab-encrusted lips.

"I guess you think its symbolic huh?" The American's deep, resonant drawl was now punctuated by a salivary lisp caused by the absence of his front teeth.

Jimmy Dolan shrugged.

"You're Catholic right? So what does this place represent to you? The remission of sins, confession, forgiveness, new beginnings? Is that why you think I brought you here?" Crook leant back and looked at the blue sky and exhaled a circle of smoke.

"I don't know...maybe."

"Ha! Horseshit!" Crook grabbed Dolan's knee and squeezed hard. "I brought you here because there's always lots of tourist pussy here Brendan. That's why! Fuck your fucking religion..."

Jimmy Dolan nodded slowly. "Okay, but seeing we're here now, and I told you my story, how about you do the same? How about I hear your confession?"

"My confession..." Crook gently ran a finger over the contours of his ruined nose, then trained his stare on a Spanish fifteen year old posing for a photo holding an ice cream.

"Like for instance, why you always call me Brendan. My name is Jimmy. Who the fuck is Brendan?"

Both men sat in silence and watched the girl, as her father positioned her alongside her mother, lining up a shot with the cathedral in the background.

Jimmy Dolan turned away, and was about to speak again, but was stopped by a sudden sob which morphed into loud, persistent weeping from the man sat alongside him. Dolan remained silent and continued to stare ahead, as Simeon Crook rocked back and forth, with his hands covering his face.

"I'm sorry. I didn't mean to..." Dolan's whispered apology was met by a raised hand from Simeon Crook, who took several deep breaths, then evacuated each nostril in turn onto the cobbled surface of Place Jean-Paul II.

"I'll tell you, okay? Just give me a minute."

Dolan watched the Spanish family walking towards Rue de la Cité as Crook began his story.

"Brendan Reid was my friend...he was like a son, no not a son. He was like my little brother. Irish boy like you, third generation though, he'd never even been there, born in Squantum Massachusetts. Met him at Langley in '66. He'd just graduated from Georgetown, part of that year's campus recruitment drive. I was a fifteen year company veteran. Ex-cop too, murder squad. I was there doing a Field Chemistry refresher course. Five days, pile of horseshit. I was teaching the instructors things they'd never even thought of. Bunch of fucking jerks..."

Simeon Crook rubbed at his nose then reached into his jacket pocket and retrieved a Gauloises packet. He removed the last cigarette, crunched the box and tossed it over his shoulder.

"Fucking jerks." Crook's hand shook as he flicked a brass Zippo lighter and teased the tobacco with the flame. Jimmy Dolan wondered if the story had ended but remained silent.

"So, anyway, the instructor on Brendan's course was an old buddy of mine, Karl Berkowitz. We were in Laos together in '63. I was living in Potomac and the kid was trying to get to ...I forget, fucking North Bethesda maybe, I don't know, some fucking shithole along the 495. Off to see some chick for the weekend, and Karl asked if I'd give him a ride. 'Sure' I said. Met him downstairs. It was about 16.00 on a Friday in late May. Sunny day, before it got too hot, perfect weather. I remember the first time I saw him. Tall, 6, maybe 6'1, built like a linebacker, fair hair, preppy clothes. You look so much like him. You could have picked Brendan out as a company man in a crowd of a thousand though. I had to smile when I saw him. I thought we need to knock that look out of him, double quick."

Simeon Crook inhaled deeply on his cigarette and closed his eyes, nodding his head and smiling as he recalled that Spring day in '66. The smile then vanished just as quickly as it had appeared as he continued his story.

"Anyways, there was a car wreck on the Georgetown Turnpike, two lanes out in each direction. We didn't move for two hours. Engine off, windows down, flicking through the stations, just shooting the breeze. The Beach Boys had just released Pet Sounds and 'Sloop John B' must have played about ten times while we sat on that freeway. My wife had just bought the album and Brendan hadn't heard it, so when we started moving again I asked him back to my place for a bite and a beer. Shit, it was too late to see his girl by then anyway."

"You were married then?" Jimmy Dolan asked the question then wished he hadn't as Crook's face fell.

"Back then, yeah. Wife, kids, house with a garden and picket fence and stars and stripes flying from the stoop. The whole nine yards..."

Crook took a last drag on his cigarette and flicked it into a flower bed.

"That's by the by...so, to cut a long story short, Brendan and I became firm friends. I'd been there, done it, he was just starting out, so I enjoyed teaching him. Things they wouldn't teach you at Langley, you know?"

Dolan nodded.

"So, time passed, the kid did well and my squad was a man down, so I recommended Brendan to my chief."

The final words of the sentence were lost to a gasp and once again, Jimmy Dolan shifted uneasily on the bench as the man next to him broke down in tears.

"Worst thing I ever did in my life..."

"But you were only trying to help Brendan, give his career a helping hand?"

Crook cleared his throat and spat hard, then turned to face Dolan.

"You don't understand son. My squad...we weren't a normal CIA unit. We were..."

"What they call Black Ops?" Dolan wondered if he shouldn't have said it, but now Crook laughed.

"Oh son, you have no fucking idea. We're talking the blackest of black ops, totally off the fucking books, 100% unauthorised, history affecting operations. And I brought Brendan in. Biggest regret of my life..."

Crook turned back to face the square and both men fell silent again, watching a tour group led by a fat man carrying a small French flag on a stick.

"We needed someone young, Brendan's age, hip enough to fit in with the Pasadena kids but plausible enough to befriend the Arab. He fit the bill perfectly."

"Who's the Arab?"

"Sirhan Sirhan. He fell under his spell immediately. Brendan told him he was a Kibbutznik who'd fallen in love with a Palestinian and defected to the PLO. He was well versed in MK-ultra techniques and basically radicalised the kid."

"Whoa, slow down...Who? You've lost me here...I have no idea what you're talking about now."

Simeon Crook smiled. "You asked and I'm telling you. If you can't keep up, that's not my problem buddy."

Jimmy Dolan shook his head as Crook continued.

"The target date was December '68 but Brendan was so good, it was brought forward six months to hit the primaries. You know the rest."

Crook stood up and stretched.

"Come on, I need some more smokes."

Jimmy Dolan stood and faced him.

"I know what? I've no idea what you just told me."

"Kennedy." Crook turned and began walking towards Cité Metro station.

"JFK? What are you saying? That Brendan arranged to have JFK killed?"

"Are you fucking stupid son?" Crook turned and walked backwards, facing Dolan. "Jack had been dead for six years by then. The brother."

"Bobby Kennedy?"

"Yeah, the fucking brother, Robert."

Jimmy Dolan's head was spinning as he hurried to catch up with Crook, who was walking briskly across the square.

"But, I don't get it, what happened to Brendan?"

Simeon Crook stopped abruptly and turned, then reached into his pocket to retrieve the Minolta camera. He raised it to his eyes and rotated the viewfinder to capture Jimmy Dolan framed against the backdrop of Notre Dame cathedral.

"Brendan did what they asked son, so they killed him. Just like I did what they asked, and now they're trying to kill me too."

# Chapter 16

**Wednesday 23 April 1975, Leeds.**

*Black Panther Hunt Switches- The hunt for the Black Panther switched back to Nottinghamshire and parts of Yorkshire today. Commander John Morrison, head of Scotland Yard's murder squad, said today that extra men had been sent to Nottingham to an area where two vehicles similar to those used by the Panther had been seen parked. He said the enquiry in Yorkshire was linked to green overalls found discarded near Bathpool Park, Kidgrove, where Lesley Whittle's body was found in a drainage shaft. The overalls had been manufactured by a company in Barnsley.*

"So you don't fancy it then?" Rita Bernard shouted from the kitchen of the terraced house on Lascelles Terrace as Alan Connolly slowly closed the net curtains, then stooped to run his fingers under the settee, feeling the cold steel of the bayonet hidden there. *Don't worry brother, it's still there. That cunt has you rattled good and proper doesn't he?*

"Shut the fuck up Keith."

"What did you say?"

Alan Connolly stared back blankly as she entered the room. "Sorry love, what were you saying?"

"Jesus Alan, what's the matter with you? Towering Inferno. It's on at 'ABC in town. It's meant to be good, do you fancy it tonight?"

"It's the Barcelona second leg tonight."

"Is it on telly?"

"No, but it's on Radio 2. Terry will have it on in the pub, I might call up there."

Rita tutted loudly and shook her head and bustled out of the room as Alan pulled back the curtain to watch a car slowly make its way along the street. *Beige Allegro brother. You're alright.. for now.*

The phone in the hall jangled suddenly, the sound echoing off the anaglypta walls.

"Hello, Leeds 621582." Rita's telephone voice usually made him smile, but her too-long pause on this occasion made his balls shrink up into his stomach.

"Yes, it is....he does. I'll get him."

Alan was already standing behind her when she turned to hand him the aubergine coloured receiver.

His hand gripped the door frame as he waited for Rita to go back into the kitchen.

"Hello."

"Alan? Is that you?"

"Who's this?"

"Colin. From Catterick."

The electrical charge sparked in his brain and his legs and stomach felt weak.

"Colin..?"

"Malcolm's son. You know, Malcolm from the landfill."

Alan Connolly inhaled deeply, the current surging in his brain and a sharp pain burning in his chest. *You know what's coming next brother.*

"Yeah, alright Colin...everything okay?"

"They've nicked my dad Alan. They came today. Won't let us see him. We got a solicitor and dad gave him your number, said we should let you know."

Alan leant his face against the living room door, lips tasting the coat of gloss Rita had applied just before Christmas.

"What did...what do they know?" His mouth was so dry he could barely form his words.

"Everything. Guns, ammo, everything. Said they were acting on a tip-off."

Fuck, Fuck, Fuck. The electricity that he thought he'd learnt to control was now sparking and fizzing again. Still wired wrong. His dead brother's laughter echoing in his mind. *You knew it was coming. They've really done a number on you this time brother.*

"Bollocks Colin, that's shit. Was it Military Police or North Yorkshire?" Connolly's mind raced. Military police would hopefully not be as quick off the mark in involving Leeds CID.

"No Alan, that's the thing, it was neither."

Alan fell silent and shifted his weight from foot to foot as Rita appeared in the doorway looking concerned and mouthing 'are you okay?'

"Who nicked him Colin?"

The line crackled and Colin began to talk about unmarked cars and armed officers and sniffer dogs.

"Colin..Colin...just tell me who it was that nicked your dad."

Colin paused to capture his breath before delivering the news that Alan Connolly didn't want to hear.

"It was Special Branch Alan, fucking Special Branch. They're treating it as terrorism. They've said my dad could be looking at twenty years."

# Chapter 17

Alan Connolly put his head down and pulled up the collar on his short-bodied leather bomber jacket as he headed down Lascelles Terrace towards Roundhay road. A man in a suit came out of the Paki shop on the corner carrying a bottle of Tizer and their eyes met.

No, 'what are you fucking looking at', today though. Alan looked away, then quickly scanned the approaching traffic on Roundhay Road. Head down, walking fast, trying to catch his breath, peering up Zetland Place, 'Young, Gifted and Black' drifting through an open window, echoing off red bricks and cobbles. Hurrying past Lowther street and the Lambtons, looking for a brown fucking Vauxhall Viva. To the corner of Harehills Lane outside the Grill and Griddle and Hernie's Hideway, into the phone box, kicking a piss-soaked yellow pages out into the street.

Finger in the dial, listening to his own breathing rebounding from the sticky curved mouthpiece of the receiver. A long double beep, two long double beeps, three long double beeps. 6pm. Imagining the barmaid, juggling Guiness pints and dodging empty pint glasses being thrust back towards her. A crowded bar of second pint drinkers, still thirsty after opening time. Four long double beeps. The Dubliners on the juke box no doubt drowning out the ringing...

'Hello Royal Oak...beepbeepbeepbeepbeep'

Alan pushed a two pence piece into the slot with his thumb.

"Hello..."

"Royal Oak." Irish brogue dripping from two words so much it sounded like a bad piss-take.

"Hello, is Lizard there?"

"Who?"

"Lizard...tell him its Alan...from Harehills. It's urgent."

The line fell silent and the faint sounds of the bar room hubbub were lost to his own heavy breathing.

"What did I tell you?" The voice on the other end of the line crackled and hissed menacingly.

"It's okay, I'm in a phonebox. I couldn't come to the pub, I think I'm being followed." Alan narrowed his eyes to peer through a cracked glass square at a brown car idling at the lights, waiting to turn right.

"Fucking hell....don't say anymore. And definitely don't come here. Meet me tomorrow at midday, the phone boxes outside the Post Office in City Square."

The line went dead with a clunk that made Alan's ears pop. He replaced the receiver and his fingers tingled and twitched with the electrical current coursing from his brain into his body, voices in his head too loud to ignore. *It's bad brother. What are you going to tell them?*

"Shut up, stop talking, let me think..." Alan tried to control his breathing and swallowed hard, his heart thumping in his chest, his face pressed against the perspex screen covering the list of dialling codes.

"Fucking Garnett Walsh. He's trying to put me out of business. Cutting everything off." *Simple solution, kill the bastard. No surrender. No fucking surrender.*

Alan Connolly shook his head and put his fingers in his ears but he knew that only made the voices louder.

"It's too late for that Keith, the damage is done." *It might be too late but it'll make you feel better, believe me.*

Alan Connolly turned and peered through the cracked glass panes of the phone box, watching a two-tone green bus pull into the traffic on Roundhay Road, its disembarked passengers vanishing in a cloud of diesel smoke.

"Walsh can wait for another day. The important thing now is to contain this before other people get dragged in. Because if that happens, it really is game over."

# Chapter 18

**Wednesday 23 April 1975, Paris.**

"Malcolm Little. You know who that is?"

Simeon Crook III swigged off the remainder of his beer and washed it down with a slug of brandy, then flicked two fingers to the waiter and nodded towards the table.

Jimmy Dolan shook his head.

"Malcolm X?"

"The black muslim. Like Muhammed Ali. Yeah I heard of him. The taught us about him at school, freedom fighter, revolutionary, all that stuff."

"Yeah well, if I look back, that's where it all started to go wrong for me with the company." Simeon Crook lit a cigarette and sat back as the sun reflected off his mirrored shades.

Jimmy Dolan didn't respond. He'd learnt to let the American speak when he was in the mood to talk about the past.

"64. I tracked that motherfucker through half of Africa. Ethiopia, Tanganiyka, Ghana, Sudan, Senegal, fucking Liberia, Algeria, Morocco. Shithole countries with bandit governments, disease ridden whores and uneatable food. Five months. Waiting for the word. Then when it finally came in Cairo, I had to work with some of Tshombe's goons. Totally fucking useless."

Jimmy Dolan smiled and shook his head.

"Riddles man. You speak in riddles. I never have a clue what you're telling me. I guess that's the point though?"

Simeon Crook paused as the waiter delivered two Kronenbourgs to the table, then drew on his cigarette again and expelled a circle of smoke which drifted across the table.

"Fucking McCone was director then. Scared to make a decision without Washington giving it the okay. Said we had to let the Congolese take the lead, even though I'd told him in no uncertain terms that they weren't up to it. Sure enough they used some kid's chemistry-set poison in his food and he tasted it. The fucker was straight out of there to get his stomach pumped out, and no surprise, he was up and about the next day."

"You got him in the end though?"

"Not us. Not me anyway. I was the fall guy for Cairo even though I was told to stay clear of the restaurant when they did it. If I'd been there it would have been a different story. And I let everyone know that. They didn't like that."

The two men fell silent as Crook finished his cigarette and immediately lit another one.

"So that's why they're trying to kill you, because they think you messed a job up?"

"No, that was just the start. That was when my star stopped rising, when they first marked my card. I was pushed into a dead-end job with Operation Mockingbird for a couple of years, but then McCone moved on and Dick Helms became director in '66. I was back on the team." Simeon Crook slurped at his beer and wiped the froth from his moustache, then picked up his zippo lighter from the table and began to slowly revolve it between his thumb and fingers.

"So why then? What did you do that's so bad that they need you out of the way?" Jimmy Dolan picked up his glass. He was getting impatient with the American's games and stared at his drink as he felt Crook turn towards him.

"To be honest, I'm not sure you're ready to know."

"Fine. Don't tell me then. To be honest I couldn't give a fuck anyway." Jimmy Dolan tipped his head back and drained his glass, then stood up as Crook continued to stare at him from his seat.

"I'm not sure you're ready to know...or even if I can trust you."

Jimmy Dolan shrugged. "Up to you..."

"Fucking sit down Jimmy." Simeon Crook removed his sunglasses and gestured towards Dolan's empty seat.

"Wow, Jimmy not Brendan, must be..."

"Serious? Yeah I'd say the murder of a friendly head of state is pretty fucking serious buddy."

Jimmy Dolan sat down. "Africa?"

"Ha, ha, some tinpot dictator of a failed state. I've done plenty of those my friend. No one cares, believe me. A key U.S. ally though? Different story..."

"Who?" Jimmy Dolan lowered his voice and leant towards Crook, who narrowed his eyes and lit another Gauloises.

"Holt. Christmas 67."

Jimmy Dolan shrugged and shook his head.

"Harry Holt, Australian prime minister. Disappeared while spear-fishing at a beach in Victoria. Body never recovered." Crook exhaled a tendril of smoke from each nostril.

"Australia? Why though?" Dolan glanced over both shoulders then leant to within a foot of Crook's face.

"It was complicated. He was getting economic heat from the Chinese, they were pressuring him to pull his troops out of Nam. We couldn't let that happen."

"So this job was a success, they couldn't say you fucked this one up?"

Crook began to laugh amidst an inhalation of tobacco smoke that caused him to break into a hacking cough which ended in a loud expulsion of phlegm onto the cobbles.

"That's the point son. I did the job I was asked to do and in doing so, I joined the long list of operatives who knew too much. Like Brendan. Like Warren Cleveland who worked with Kubrick on the moon landings. Like Jim Palmer who ran the regime change in Indonesia. Like with Castro, Lumumba, Trujillo. Our guys all had their orders. Some happened, some didn't, but the bosses didn't care, they still knew too much. Nixon called it cleaning the stable. To them we were just shit that needed shovelling out." Crook inhaled deeply and the cigarette end glowed orange and he put back on his sunglasses.

"So...what did you do?"

"What did we do? Those of us that could, got out. Went underground. Self-employed. Formed our own 'company', using the skills we were taught by the U.S. Government. There are a dozen of us, a few are still in the States but most of us are scattered around the world. Meet the Western Europe representative of RAD Team." Simeon Crook smiled and extended his hand across the table.

"RAD Team?" Jimmy Dolan took Crook's hand and winced as the American crunched his fingers.

"R.A.D. Retired, Angry, Dangerous. That's us. And we don't come cheap, because believe me Brendan, we're the absolute best in the world at what we do."

# Chapter 19

**Thursday 24 April 1975, Leeds.**

*United's Dream Nears Reality- The incredible Billy Bremner did not stop running at the triumphant end of Leeds United's match in Barcelona. He kept right on, weaving and jinking his way across the crowded pitch. The little man had run himself into the ground for 90 minutes but he was determined to share his moment of joy with the United supporters who had followed their team to Spain. In front of the faithfuls at last, he jumped for joy, beating the air with his fists in exultation. As the tiny United band, who had raised their voices amid the Spanish multitude, cheered and cheered again.*

Alan Connolly sat on a bench outside Leeds Central Post Office in City Square, flanked by the bronze figures of James Watt and John Harrison, and folded the Evening Post in two so he could read the back page. He twisted and craned his neck to see the clock tower behind him. Five to twelve. He scanned the square ahead of him. A middle aged woman pulled a tartan shopping trolley and a man in a beige suit paused to tie a shoelace beneath the plumed tail of the Black Prince's horse.

Steve had dropped him off outside Chelsea Girl after doing two Vicar Lane-Boar Lane-Briggate circuits to make sure they weren't being followed. Alan had then taken a quick left up the cobbled street past the City Varieties and the Piccadilly bar, then left down Lands Lane past the new Schofield's building site. He'd paused to look in Harry Fenton's window to check the reflections of people passing behind him, then joined the shuffling queue in Hagenbachs, just long enough to check the street beyond the plate glass windows. A right turn up Commercial Street, and across Albion Street then ducking into Yates's Wine Lodge doorway, pausing for breath, scanning left and right along Bond Street. Then left on Park Row next to the Labour Exchange, down into City Square, through the door of RS.Mcolls, pretending to look at the magazines while he scanned the square, then picking up a YEP, handing over the 2p, and crossing the road, heart beating hard. Switch flicked, electricity surging, current buzzing in his head, into his veins. Still wired wrong. *Calm down brother or you're going to fuck this up.*

Alan Connolly now pushed his back into the hard contours of the bench, inhaled through his mouth and breathed slowly out through his nose, feeling his chest rising and falling. The man in the beige suit patted down his lapels, then lit a cigarette and walked towards Boar Lane, and Alan watched green two tone buses jockeying for position at the stops in the shadow of the dark stone façade of the Queens Hotel.

A movement to his left caused Alan to turn, as the man known as the Lizard sat down on the bench next to him. Wearing a blue anorak with red and white bands on the arms he looked straight ahead and bit at his lower lip with yellow incisor teeth.

"Alright?" Alan didn't look at him as he spoke.

"What do you fucking think? Get on with it, what do you want?"

Alan Connolly puffed out his cheeks. "We've got a problem."

"I don't like problems Alan." The man now turned to face him, breathing old tobacco from two feet away.

"I know, I'm sorry." Alan turned his head towards the wide, square face with bloated cheeks that rendered the Lizard's ears invisible and gave him his nickname.

"My bloke at Catterick's been lifted."

The Lizard sniffed and shuffled his feet. "So what's that mean?"

"Well, it means no more deliveries obviously..."

"For fuck's sake Alan!" A woman carrying a parcel towards the Post Office door turned towards them then quickly looked away and the Lizard lowered his voice. "You can't do that. You've made commitments."

"What can I do? The army aren't going to use him again even if he gets out. It's fucked, the whole thing."

"Jesus, Alan." The Lizard shook his head and rubbed at his temples.

"Think you can square it away with the Manchester lot?"

"I've absolutely no idea, but they aren't going to be happy, I can tell you that. This bloke isn't likely to talk is he? Who nicked him, military police?" Tobacco breath on his cheek again but Alan kept looking across City Square at two men folding Lino outside Eastern Carpet Stores.

"Erm, yeah I think it was Army police."

"Will he keep quiet? He's only a farmer isn't he?"

"Yeah, yeah, farm and landfill site, he'll keep quiet, I'm sure of it."

The Lizard stood up and looked down at Alan. "Well he better do. Because if he doesn't, me and you will be joining him in that fucking landfill, and that's a promise."

# Chapter 20

**Saturday 26 April 1975, Leeds.**

*Spend, Spend, Spend to Beat the Budget- It was Spend, spend, spend in Yorkshire today as shoppers scrambled to beat Chancellor Dennis Healey's budget increases on luxuries ranging from colour TV sets to bottles of wine. Leeds stores reported a big business boom in the rush to buy now and save later. The Bank of England stepped in to support the pound on foreign exchanges as it fell as low as £2.38 against the dollar. The concern was the short term inflationary shock of the budget.*

"Thirty of us at 'top of 'South Bank. Got in early and went straight to 'back, like you always tell us Alan, and when they came up 'steps we just piled down into 'em. Should have seen them run..." Max's mate Geoff was holding the attention of the senior members of the LS9 Asylum who were assembled around two tables in the far corner of the Three Legs.

"Why has Maxie got a black eye if you turned them over?" Dennis Copley smiled as Max pushed through the crowd from the bar clutching two pints of Tetley's.

"This were from after." Max placed the glasses amongst a table full of empties and rubbed at a swelling on his eyebrow. "They couldn't shift us in 'ground but they were waiting for us outside. We were well outnumbered but me and Geoff didn't run."

"Not till all 'others did anyway." Geoff chipped in, causing Max to shake his head and scowl.

"If you lot had been there we'd have cleared that whole end, I'm telling you. Thirty of us in there, all well game and 'oldest lad there were only 23."

"Bigger fish to fry than Wolves for a game that means nowt. Armfield even played that Welsh kid Harris at nine didn't he?" Dennis Copley turned to Alan without waiting for Max to reply. "Heard owt about 'bus for Paris Alan?"

"I've told Budgie we need a forty-seater, he's trying to sort a driver who'll do three days. He's saying none of them want to sleep on the bus so we might have to pay for a couple of nights digs for whoever does it."

"What's the plan then?"

The tables fell silent as Alan outlined the agenda.

"I'm thinking we set off from the Waterloo Monday night. Drive down and get the ferry early next morning. Into Paris Tuesday lunchtime. Gives us plenty of time to sort tickets. Two nights in Paris, then set off back on Thursday morning. Back here Thursday night."

"Do we need a hotel then?" Geoff swayed as he slurped on his pint.

"Nah, fuck that. We can either kip on the bus or in a strip club."

"Leeds are only getting 8,000 tickets. We've no chance of getting any from them." Max pulled a stool up to the table and sat down.

"Unless we can get a load of tokens." Norman muttered under his breath and cast a sideways glance towards Alan.

"Fuck off Norm." Alan mouthed his reply silently.

"Touts will have plenty of tickets, don't you worry." Dennis Copley stood up holding an empty glass and pushed his way towards the bar.

"Yeah how much will they be asking though?" Geoff was shaking his head when Copley's grinning face appeared over his shoulder.

"Who cares what they're asking! We won't be paying, we're the fucking Asylum, we don't pay for owt!"

The cheers and laughter had barely subsided when Steve Bernard's afro curls appeared through the crowd and he caught Alan's eye and summoned him with an upward nod of the head.

As he approached, Alan saw Steve scanning the faces at the tables and knew he was assessing the strength of the force available, and immediately felt his heartbeat quicken.

"What's up?"

"Walsh's lads in 'Strega. Four of them. Came in when it opened at nine."

"Selling?"

Steve nodded. "Set up at a table in 'back room. We had a couple of young lads in. That big bastard, Kennedy, pulled a baseball bat out of his coat and told them to fuck off."

"No Walsh though?"

"No, he's in 'Hayfield. I sent someone up to have a look. There's a good few of them in there and there'll be more when 'Nash shuts."

Alan leant on the bar and glanced back towards the table.

"Nigel's on the door at Cinderella's till two. Half of this lot are too pissed to be of any use. We're short-handed."

"And it could be a trap. Once you're in 'Strega, there's no easy way out."

"Or the four of them might just have taken a flyer. Walsh might not have told them to go there." Alan rubbed at his chin. *Benefit of the doubt brother? You're going fucking soft man.*

"Fuck it, come on. Dennis, pass my coat."

Dennis Copley passed the leather trenchcoat over the table and Alan Connolly pulled it on, and ran his hand down the length of the bayonet in the lining.

"Who are we taking?" Steve paused and looked back towards the table.

"No one. Just me and you." Alan Connolly pushed his way through the last-orders crowd at the bar and out onto the Headrow, electrical current surging, fizzing through his veins again, his brother's laughter filling his mind. *Here we go. Here we fucking go brother. No surrender. No fucking surrender.*

## Chapter 21

The two men climbed silently into Steve's Avenger parked outside the Three Legs. Up the Headrow and a right turn along Upper Briggate past Lewis's and the Harehills bus queues, The Tower showing 'Death Wish' and The Plaza deviating from its usual tits and bush schedule with a screening of 'The Exorcist'.

Alan Connolly broke the silence at the Wren's red light.

"I can't let it go Steve. Not after what's happened."

A nod and a sigh in response, then silence all the way to Sheepscar lights.

"Is 'farmer out yet?"

"I don't know Steve, I've not heard anything and I've no way to contact him. He better keep his fucking mouth shut though. If I get pulled in, I don't know what this Manchester firm will do. Obviously I'll keep quiet, but they don't know me. They might try to cut the risk, just to make sure." Alan ran his fingers along the hard steel in the lining of his coat, hearing his own breathing, too fast above the idling engine.

Heart beating hard in his chest as the Avenger travelled up Roundhay Road, past the end of his street.

"What time's Rita finish?" Steve was trying to make conversation but instead only summoned images in Alan's mind of his girlfriend dancing in a cage in the Peel for the amusement of Fat Trevor and his pals. *That's good brother, hold that thought.*

"Put it in the Fordy car park."

Steve pulled up alongside the painted sign which read 'Man O'War bar,' that no one had ever understood but now seemed to make perfect sense.

"What's the plan...?" Steve hadn't even turned the key in the ignition before Alan was out of the car, jogging across the car park, jumping the small wall. Steve's voice behind him, telling him to wait, that he was coming. Dodging between a Toyota Corolla and a Transit van with a single working headlight, over the barrier, down the slope, 'Johnny Too Bad' by the Slickers escaping the basement out onto the streets, where it belonged. Down the steps, kicking the door till old Gladstone slid back the bolt.

"Alan..."

"Don't ask me to sign in tonight mate, I was never here...and leave the door open."

Jean caught his eye from behind the bar, pushing cans of Red Stripe and Breaker through the grill to a lanky kid with short dreads and a long spliff. Faces at a table on the right, paused mid conversation as they saw him come through the door , crossing the dancefloor, *walking down the road with a ratchet in your waist, Johnny you're too bad...* A fat bleach-blonde hooker staggering in his path was guided aside by his left forearm. Kennedy and two other black lads were sat at a table in the corner, his big smile lit up, flashing with the lights. Purple, red, green. Nodding his head, grinning like fucking Bingo off the Banana Splits. Another black kid approached from the right and put down his drink, fumbling in his jacket pocket as Kennedy stood up, still smiling, tilting his head from side to side, shrugging his shoulders, loosening himself up. *No Prisoners brother. You know the score.* Garnett Walsh. Rita in a cage. Lizard. Manchester Mob.

Fat Trevor. A Catterick farmer. Special Branch. *We've been here before. No fucking prisoners.*

The lights flashed, purple, red, green. *One of these days when you hear a voice say come, where you gonna run to...* The electrical charge levelled out and his breathing slowed, his heart beating in time with the lilting rhythm blasting from the speakers.

The kid on the right was holding a hammer which he dropped as the bayonet pierced his Prince of Wales checked trousers just below the twenty button waistband. Kennedy was off and running, not grinning anymore, and he collided with a table filled with empty Red Stripe cans, sending it spinning across the dancefloor with a clatter. Screams replaced the music and the room lights flickered on, as Kennedy's thick platform soles skidded on the wet surface and he sprawled, legs apart like a baby deer on ice. Alan scowled towards Darren on the DJ Stand and the turntable scratched back into life with the plaintive trumpet intro of 'You Can Get it if you Really Want' drowning out Kennedy's pleading cries.

Alan flashed the blade at the other two black lads who were helping the kid in the blood-soaked checked trousers to his feet.

"We just came for a drink Alan, we're off to a party in Roundhay. Honest, we only sold a bit of weed to some lasses who asked us. We weren't taking 'piss, honestly. Please..."

Kennedy pushed himself backwards along the floor until he reached the bar, where he sat, legs splayed in front of him, his chest rising and falling and his bulging eyes focused on the blade which was now hovering an inch from his nose.

"Please Alan, no..." Kennedy's lip quivered and he closed his eyes as Alan lifted the bayonet and carefully positioned the point between his eyes then gently jabbed once, causing a thin rivulet of blood to trickle down into his eye and down his cheek, and a quickly expanding patch of wet to appear in the crotch of his brush-denim jeans.

Alan slowly lifted the bayonet and observed a splash of blood on the blade in the flashing lights, then lowered it again and wiped it on Kennedy's cheesecloth shirt, then slid it back into his trenchcoat.

"You tell Walsh... what he's done...it's not alright. And I won't forget. Ever."

Alan Connolly turned and crossed the dancefloor, signalling to Darren to pass him the microphone. Desmond Dekker scratched to an immediate halt and a screech of feedback preceded Alan speaking, with the lights flashing in response to each word he spoke.

"Apologies for the minor disturbance ladies and gents. Normal service will now resume, and hopefully you'll quickly forget this unfortunate incident. In fact..I KNOW you'll forget this unfortunate incident." Alan scanned the faces in the room then handed the microphone back to the DJ.

"Enjoy the rest of your night folks."

# Chapter 22

**Thursday 1 May 1975, Paris.**

*Cheaper to live in North claim – The cost of living gap between the south of England and Yorkshire is steadily narrowing, although it is still cheaper to live in the north, a report has revealed. One of the main reasons for the trend is said to be house prices, which have escalated in West Yorkshire by up to 10% in the past 6 months, with a particular rise in the price of mid-tier homes. A three bedroom semi in Leeds for example has gone up from an average £8,000 in October 1974 to £8,800 in March this year. However, the cost of a £24,000 detached home has remained the same according to the Economic Trends report published by West Yorks County Council.*

"Fuck's sake." Gerry Cleary looked at his watch and hammered on the door of the attic apartment in Pigalle for the third time, then pushed his ear to the door in response to muffled sounds from within the room.

The lock clicked and the door slowly swang open and the face of a red-eyed, middle aged man blinked back at him.

Cleary looked the man up and down. Late forties or early fifties, he had unkempt shoulder length hair and a droopy, greying moustache. His open shirt revealed prominent ribs and an eagle tattoo on his chest. His nose seemed recently broken and his cheek and eye sockets bore signs of old bruises.

"And who the fuck might you be?"

"I might ask you the same." The deep drawl revealed the man to be an American, and the stench of alcohol on his breath betrayed a heavy drinking session. His missing front teeth did nothing to dispel Cleary's initial view that the man was a down and out.

"Where's Jimmy? I'm here with his money."

The American swayed in the doorway, then belched loudly and opened the door to allow Cleary into the flat.

A shape beneath a pink blanket in the bed stirred and shuffled, and eventually the crumpled face of Jimmy Dolan appeared from beneath the covers, as the American clung to the fridge door and poured himself a drink from a spirit bottle on the sink.

"You want one?"

"It's ten o'clock in the morning for God's sake!" Cleary shook his head as Dolan seemed to recognise him for the first time.

"Ah Gerry, it's you! What day is it?"

"It's the first of May Jimmy, I've brought your cash."

"Thanks Gerry, yeah, first of May, what day is it though?"

"Jesus Christ Jimmy." Gerry Cleary looked round the room as the American slumped in an armchair with the glass of spirit, then pulled a green blanket over himself. Cans and bottles littered the floor and a purple towel served as a curtain over a small, cracked window. A bin in the corner of the room disgorged takeaway containers and a small table was piled high with unwashed crockery.

"Just what the fuck is going on here?"

Jimmy Dolan looked around the room and shrugged and the American began to laugh quietly.

"What's going on here buddy is that Jimmy and I are on vacation in Paris. We're having a good time. Lifting him out of the depression he's been wallowing in."

"Who is this man Jimmy?" Gerry Cleary approached the bed where Jimmy Dolan sat, rubbing at his matted hair with soiled hands.

"Simeon Crook III, at your service sir..." The American extended his hand from the armchair and Gerry Cleary took a step back. "And don't you worry, although we may appear to be having a wild old time at present, I'll be getting Jimmy back on the straight and narrow very soon. Yessir, the vacation is almost over. I've got some serious business to attend to here in Paris very soon and I'll be needing this young man on top form to help me out."

The American grinned a gap toothed smile through scabbed, cracked lips and stood to attention and saluted.

Gerry Cleary turned back to the figure slumped in the bed.

"I'm going to have to report back on this I'm afraid Jimmy. For God's sake son, you need to sort yourself out!"

# Chapter 23

**Monday 6 May 1975, Leeds.**

*Pound Falls again – Holidaymakers bound for France, West Germany and Switzerland were again hit today as the pound plumbed to record depths on foreign exchange markets. It dropped to a new low of around 9.3 francs at one time in Paris—a fall of 30 centimes in the last week. On the West German exchange in Frankfurt it also fell to its lowest level of 5386 marks, which is a pfennig lower than its closing rate last night.*

Normally, Alan Connolly hated the sound of his brother's mocking laugh, echoing in his head, but now, lying on the cold floor of a speeding van, his hands tied behind his back and a hessian sack over his head, it felt almost comforting.

*You always knew it would come to this brother. From when we were wee boys in Glasgow, this was always how it would finish. At least you'll go out in a blaze of glory. Not topping yourself in some fucking high security nut house with no ears, fingers or teeth like this poor old fucker!*

The men hadn't spoken when they'd put him in the van. Steve had offered him a lift from the Waterloo but then Cockney Pete had bought him another drink and Alan had wanted to get off home. He'd spotted the blue Commer van with a white roof parked in one of the Bayswaters as he'd walked along Harehills Road. He spotted anything out of the ordinary now. Any car parked up with the lights on, driving too slow, too fast, any brown cars. Then they'd caught him out with a classic diversion tactic. A Vauxhall Viva parked on the corner of

Conway Mount, interior lights on, two figures in the front seats. He'd been looking over his shoulder, keeping tabs on that as he'd turned into Elford Grove, and there it was again, seen too late, that fucking Commer van. He'd paused, wondering if he was imagining it, but if he turned back he was heading straight towards the Viva.

By the time he'd decided to carry on, they were out, charging over the road towards him, three masked men, one with a pistol pointing at his head. Knocked him down, bag on his head, thrown in the back. Lying there now he thought he might have dislocated his shoulder as he couldn't feel his arm anymore. He thought about Rita. Night off tonight and she'd wanted to go to the pictures again. Still not seen that 'Towering Inferno'. Sounded shite but he'd give anything to be there now. In the ABC on Vicar Lane drinking Kia-Ora and eating a tub of overpriced ice cream. Instead he was bagged up and tied up, on his way to what? *Fucks sake brother, stop your fucking greeting. Man up and meet what's coming. Die a soldier's death. Look 'em in the fucking eye and tell 'em, no surrender!*

He couldn't work out how long he'd been in the van or which direction they'd taken. He guessed at about half an hour as he now couldn't feel his feet, couldn't even move them with what felt like washing line wrapped around his knees and ankles. He strained to hear any sounds from inside or outside the van, but there was nothing beyond the engine and a squeaking brake pad. No talking, no clue as to who had taken him. Walsh. The Manchester Firm. Special Branch. He didn't know which would be worse, and suddenly felt like he was going to puke and was glad they hadn't gagged him. A new sound brought him back into the van...the repetitive click of an indicator preceded a sharp braking which propelled him forward, then a wide arc as the driver executed a full-lock turn.

Then different tyre sounds, the rumble of rubber on gravel and a sudden slowing as the van lurched through pot-holes before coming to a halt. The ratchet creak of the handbrake being applied caused his stomach to lurch, and again he fought the urge to vomit. The rear doors creaked open and he was hauled backwards by his feet then pulled upright by two pairs of arms and dragged over rough ground, his oxblood 'Royals' scraping along the gravel.

The sound of a padlock and chain being uncoupled was followed by the creak of large wooden doors being opened, then the smell of damp and engine oil. He could hear muffled voices now. Older men, probably white, which ruled out Walsh. Too professional too. He was pushed down onto a hard chair and someone began to run a thick rope around his torso, securing him to the chair back. Now he was glad his legs were tied so tightly as it prevented them shaking uncontrollably. His stomach felt like it had liquified and he tightened his sphincter to maintain control of his bowels. *Die like a soldier brother. Don't give them the satisfaction of watching you shit yourself.*

Once tied to the chair with the rope tight against his ribs, he sensed the three men stepping back to observe him, to satisfy themselves that he was secure. One straightened the bag and he half imagined that the hand rested on his head for just a semi-second too long, perhaps trying to reassure him, comfort him maybe, ahead of what was to come. *Bollocks brother. These boys are killers. Think they give a fuck about you? All they're thinking about is how long it's going to take to dig the hole to bury you.*

Then suddenly they were gone. The sound of the wooden doors scraping the floor, then the chain and padlock rattling told him he was alone. He shivered. It felt like he was in a cave, clearly some sort of industrial unit without windows, where the warmth of Spring was still far away. His shoulder ached and his toes were numb but at least he could feel them again. He contemplated trying to move but worked out that if he tipped the chair over he could be lying face down and doubled up for hours. Days even. *That's if they come back at all. Maybe they'll just leave you here, let you starve slowly. Fuck brother, that would be a shitty way to go.*

"Shut the fuck up Keith."

His brother laughed in his head.

"Always there aren't you? Just chipping away. Never anything useful. Just helping me make bad decisions." *Ah so it's all my fault now is it?*

"You wind me up. Start me off. You always have. Even when I was a kid." *I more or less brought you up, ya ungrateful wee cunt.*

"And you made a cracking job of that didn't you?" With a hessian sack over his head, tied to a chair and awaiting an unknown fate in a cold, damp industrial unit, Alan Connolly laughed, long and hard. Harder than he'd laughed for a long time.

"Glad you're enjoying yourself there." The voice came from directly in front of him and caused an electrical charge to race through his veins. He felt the hairs on his head and arms stand on end in response to the sudden static charge, and his heart beat so hard it felt like it would burst from his rib cage.

The bag was pulled roughly from his head and he blinked in the blue glow of a strip light high above. The man holding the bag looked down at him and held out a bottle of water which he tipped forward towards Alan's mouth.

"Was that your brother you were talking to?" Alan gulped at the water then turned his head towards the voice, calm, quiet and unmistakably Irish. A man in his sixties with white hair framing a high forehead, sat on a hardbacked chair in front of the large wooden doors.

"I heard how he died. That you still talk to him. Some people think that's strange. If it brings you some comfort, I don't see a problem with it."

Alan coughed and water dribbled down his chin. The man standing alongside him moved behind him, out of sight

"Who are you?" Alan tried and failed to control the tremor in his voice.

The man with the white hair sniffed and leaned forward, resting his palms on his thighs.

"We're the people you've left with a situation, now your friend the farmer has been nicked."

"From Manchester?" At least Alan now knew who he was dealing with.

"Well sort of..." The man narrowed his eyes and nodded slightly as if weighing Alan up. "What did the Lizard tell you about us?"

Alan shrugged. "Nothing really. Just said you were a firm out of Manchester."

"So..." The man with the white hair paused, as if deciding whether he was being lied to. "You don't know who you've been selling military surplus to for the last six months?"

"I was just told it was a Manchester firm. I didn't want to know any more, didn't need to. I was just the connection between the old guy who had access to the hardware and...people who needed it."

"And you didn't think to enquire why they needed it?" The man with the white hair leant back in the chair, his eyes boring into Alan's.

"Didn't matter to me."

"Didn't matter..." The man with the white hair looked over Alan's shoulder and smiled. "You're from Glasgow?"

"Aye, been down here ten years, but spent most of that time in the nick. Can you untie me?"

"Soon. What side are you?"

"Football? Celtic but Leeds now."

"I didn't mean that but you answered anyway. Catholic then?"

"Well, I haven't been to Mass for a long time but yeah as a kid I was."

"Are you a sympathiser?" The man with the white hair folded his arms and lifted his chin slightly.

"Am I a what?"

The man looked over Alan's shoulder again and smirked.

"Are...you...sympathetic....to the cause Alan?"

"The cause..."Alan's mouth fell open and his head began to spin as the realisation dawned as to who he was dealing with. *Fuck me brother. Grandad would have been proud of you. You've become a freedom fighter...*

"I...I'm not really into anything like that, not bothered about politics or religion."

"Not into politics or religion eh? Well, I think you are now son, whether you like it or not. I hear it's the Branch?

"What? What is?"

"Special Branch. Who've nicked the farmer...That's what I'm hearing from our man on the inside."

"I don't know anything about that. His son just said he'd got lifted..."

"Yeah well, if it's right, and he's some fucking old carrot cruncher with no form, he's not going to last long before he breaks is he?"

Alan felt the presence of the man behind him, before a hand came to rest on his left shoulder.

"And when he breaks, as he surely will, that will lead them straight to you won't it?" The white haired man nodded and Alan felt the pressure on his shoulder increase.

"He doesn't really know me, he's only got a phone number." *You know where this is going brother. You're a risk. A loose end that needs tying up.*

"A phone number is no problem to the Branch son. I'm guessing they know your address already. Have you noticed anyone watching you?" The white haired man stood up and stretched slowly.

"No, no one. I've been careful."

The white haired man turned towards the wooden doors and paced back and forth.

"So, you see my problem Alan. I don't know you. You're about to get nicked and I don't know if I can trust you."

"Yeah you can, I told you, I've done loads of time, been interviewed for 24 hours non-stop by Leeds Murder Squad, I said nothing. Ever."

The white haired man turned back towards him and nodded and smiled.

"Yes, I've done my homework on you Alan. My first inclination was to clip you straight off. No risk then. But I asked around. I'm aware of your record, your experience. I'm told you're sound enough. I've also been made aware of your leisure time interests."

"Leisure time?" Alan recoiled as the man behind him now placed a hand on his right shoulder and squeezed again.

"Football. You're one of these hooligans I hear. Bovver Boys is it?" The white haired man smiled and raised his eyebrows like an interested primary school teacher.

"Well, yeah, me and the boys sometimes have a bit of a tear-up at the match."

"Leeds United fan. Wee Billy Bremner. Johnny Giles. Jackie Charlton."

"He's retired Michael." The sudden voice from behind Alan made him flinch.

"Whatever. Nasty buggers, but they could play a bit. And now...Paris!" The white haired man spread his arms wide and smiled. "European Cup Final!"

"Yeah, end of the month."

"You'll be taking a bus."

"Well, that's the plan, I'm just...."

"It wasn't a question Alan. I was telling you. You will be taking a bus."

"Right. Yes. Of course. I'm trying to get a 40-seater."

The white haired man pulled the chair closer and sat down facing Alan.

"That's good. You'll take a 40 seater, and you'll sell 39 places to your gang. That's all. Understand?"

Alan flinched at the feel of cold steel on his neck as the man behind him began to cut through the washing line.

"Yes fine, I'll sell 39 places. Can I ask why I shouldn't fill the bus?"

The white haired man leant forward and squeezed Alan's knee.

"On the way, you'll have a spare seat. On the way back, you won't. Understand?"

The white haired man smiled and winked.

"We'll be in touch very soon Alan. Welcome to the team."

# Chapter 24

**Saturday 10 May 1975, Paris.**

*Food Rationing warning – Housewives were warned today that food rationing may be introduced if prices continue to rise. Mr Tom Lynch, president of the National Union of Shopkeepers urged the government to introduce price controls now. He also said that to stop food hoarding by warehouses, large retailers and housewives, consideration may have to be given to distribution control. 'This will become imperative to ensure fair shares of food stocks are given to all' he told the Union's annual conference in Buxton.*

"Come on Crook, let me come. I've always wanted to visit Marseille. You can take care of your business then we can head down to St.Tropez!" Jimmy Dolan swigged off his beer and signalled to the waiter for a refill.

"I'm sorry buddy, but this is important RAD team business. I can use you later but no outsiders at this point."

The waiter appeared and looked disparagingly at the two men as he picked up Dolan's glass.

"Two more Pierre."

"Not for me thanks." Simeon Crook raised a hand and held it over his half full glass.

"What the fuck man! What's got into you?" Jimmy Dolan shook his head and flicked a crumpled serviette across the table.

"I've been activated Jimmy. So for me, the vacation is over." Crook removed a cigarette from a pack on the table and tapped it three times on his palm before slowly lifting it to his mouth where it remained unlit.

"Fucking activated! What's that mean anyway?"

Crook removed the cigarette from his mouth and jabbed it towards the young Irishman as he spoke.

"It means I have had instructions, so now I'm active. I'm working. And I need to go to Marseille for a few days. Your job is to slow down, clean yourself up, and get ready. I'm going to need you here and on top form in a couple of weeks. Can I rely on you Jimmy?"

"Yeah, sure...." Dolan slumped in his seat and looked away.

"I said, can I rely on you Jimmy? Can I really, really rely on you? Because make no mistake, this is serious business, and if I can't depend on you 101%, I'm going to have to cut you loose son."

"Yeah, fuck it, yeah. You can rely on me Crook, I won't let you down."

"Good boy, Jimmy. Now smile. Last photo to remember our vacation." Simeon Crook levelled the Minolta camera and twisted the viewfinder and clicked two shots.

"I'll be back by the end of next week, all being well."

# Chapter 25

**Monday 12 May 1975, Leeds.**

*Girls in Osmonds' Riot – Police quelled a mini riot when 200 teenyboppers tried to mob the Osmonds pop group in London today after tracking them down to their secret headquarters in exclusive Eton Square, Belgravia. The fans, all young girls, attempted to break through barriers when members of the group were spotted on a balcony. After four minutes of pandemonium, 10 girls were carried away in a state of collapse. Scores more were left weeping on the pavement.*

"We'll have to call this our bench if we ever get married." The Lizard smiled at his own bad joke as he sat down next to Alan Connolly outside the Post Office in City Square.

Alan Connolly stared ahead, watching a black and white Evening Post van deliver a bundle of papers to McColls.

"You're a cunt. And you're lucky I don't fucking slice you open."

"Nice to see you too Alan." The Lizard puffed out his cheeks and unzipped his blue anorak. "Quite warm in the sun..."

"Just get on with it will you. I presume you have my instructions from the fucking Provos."

"Ah so that's what you've got the hump about...I thought it was best you didn't know."

"Best I didn't know! You fucking wanker!" Alan stood up and clenched his fists as the Lizard looked down at his own feet. "Do you know what happened? What they did to me?"

"Calm down Alan. Sit down. You're attracting attention." The Lizard scanned the square and nodded and smiled to an old woman counting out a book of green shield stamps.

"Don't tell me to calm down. You fucking stitched me up. I'd have never sold stuff to them if I'd known." Alan stood over the Lizard, a vein twitching in his forehead, trying to control his breathing and quieten his brother's voice in his head. *Walk away brother. Then do the cunt outside the Royal Oak at closing. Too many witnesses here.*

"You shut the fuck up!" Alan turned and snapped at no one and the old woman with the stamps flinched.

"I didn't say anything Alan. Please just sit down. Calm down..." The Lizard patted the bench and continued staring down at his Clark's Hush Puppies. "Come on, let me explain. I didn't tell you for a reason."

"Yeah because you knew what I'd say. Why would I risk getting 25 fucking years for them?"

The Lizard patted the bench again and Alan sat down, shaking his head .

"I didn't tell you to protect you, if the farmer got nicked. I thought that if he went down, your name would be straight in the frame. If I could tell the 'Ra that you didn't know anything, you were protected. If they thought you knew, they'd have hit you in whatever maximum security nick they put you in. That's what their little test was about."

"Test? Being bagged up and thrown in a van was a test?"

"I'm not sure but I guess so. I told them you had no idea who the end buyer was, beyond some mob in Manchester. I guess they wanted to look you in the eye to see if that was true. I'm glad you convinced them, or I'd have been the next one in the back of that van."

"Fucking hell Lizard. I'm out of my depth here." Alan Connolly rested his chin on his fist and watched a toddler scatter the pigeons in the shadow of the Black Prince.

"You and me both lad. I'm too old for this." Lizard forced a smile and nudged Alan with his shoulder. "You still not heard anything about the farmer then?"

"Nope, nothing. Over two weeks now since they nicked him. I can't work it out. I've been kipping in my clothes since then, expecting the early morning knock."

"Well, maybe the old fella is tougher than we thought. Maybe he's kept his mouth shut."

Both men fell silent again.

"So, next bit of bad news...what is it they want me to do?"

The Lizard fumbled in the pocket of his anorak and handed Alan a folded piece of paper.

"What's this?"

"You're to ring it when you get to Paris on your football trip. Ask for Gerry."

"Is that who they want me to bring back on the bus?"

The Lizard screwed up his face and bit his lower lip while shaking his head. "Again, Alan, I'd say you probably don't want to know..."

"For fuck's sake! No then. The answer is no. I'm not doing it unless I know who, or what, is coming back on my bus, and why." Alan stood up and thrust his hands into the pockets of his leather jacket and stared down at the Lizard, who grimaced and squinted up at the top floor of Royal Exchange house, first skyscraper of the motorway city.

"You can't say no Alan, it's not an option. You made a commitment and didn't deliver. You owe them now."

"Alright. But I need to know. Please." Alan sat down and both men stared silently as the toddler's mother spanked his legs, causing his screams to fill the square.

Eventually, the Lizard sighed and spoke quietly.

"Okay. He's what they're calling a missing soldier. His name is Jimmy Dolan."

"That's a start. Who is he? Why is he missing?"

The Lizard took a deep inhalation and exhaled loudly.

"Fucking hell Alan."

"Just tell me. I need to know."

"M62 Coach bombing last year." The Lizard spat the words then scratched at his thinning hair while chewing at his lip again.

"Jesus Christ. Fucking hell. What, he was the one who blew it up?" Alan Connolly turned to face the Lizard, mouth open and eyes wide in horror.

"He transported the bomb. I don't think he knew what it was for. I really don't know, and that's the truth."

"Oh Jesus. Fuck, fuck, fuck." Alan Connolly put his head in his hands and rocked back and forth on the bench as the Lizard continued. *Fucking child killers now brother. Terrorists. There's no coming back from this one.*

"They got him out of the country on someone else's passport. He's been in Paris for the last year but they've heard he's fallen in with some mad Yank. Pissed every night, living like a tramp, getting into trouble. The 'Ra are scared he's going to get lifted over there and blow the whole thing open...pardon the pun." The Lizard cracked a half smile but Alan Connolly had missed the joke.

"So where do I fit in?"

"Ten thousand Leeds fans crossing the channel on buses and trains. After the match they'll just want rid of you as quick as possible at the ports. They aren't going to check everyone's passport photos are they? The Provos reckon he'll breeze through unnoticed on a bus full of lads who've been on the ale for two days."

"Then what?"

"This bloke Gerry will tell you where to drop him. Some 'A' Road in Kent. They'll pick him up from there."

Alan Connolly closed his eyes and rubbed at his temples. *Babysitting a bomber. You've really hit the big time now.*

"It could be a lot worse Alan. They could have asked you to carry guns or drugs back. That would be a lot more dangerous. I'd say it's a pretty good plan, low risk. Then it's over. Your debt is paid and you walk away."

Alan Connolly nodded. "I'll do it. One question."

"Go on."

"What if this Jimmy Dolan likes it in Paris with his American friend? What if he doesn't want to come home?"

The Lizard stood slowly and patted Alan on the shoulder.

"They've made it very clear Alan, you WILL bring him back, whether he wants to or not."

"But if he won't though?" Alan looked up, squinting as the sun broke through the permanent blanket of thick grey cloud above the Queen's Hotel.

"Then you'll have to make him. I'm afraid it's him or you lad. Good luck." The Lizard raised his right hand to wave over his shoulder, then zipped up his anorak and walked away across City Square without looking back.

# Chapter 26

**Friday 16 May 1975, Paris.**

*Casual Ali Retains Title in round 11- A lethargic Muhammed Ali, who seemed to be in danger of letting his world heavyweight title slip away, suddenly awoke with a non-stop barrage of punches to stop challenger Ron Lyle in the 11$^{th}$ round of their fight in Las Vegas early today. After the fight was stopped Ali turned to the crowd and punched the air and shouted 'I am the greatest, I am the greatest!'*

"You're in a good mood tonight, so you are." Jimmy Dolan leant towards Simeon Crook as his zippo lighter tickled the end of Dolan's fat Cuban cigar.

As the tip glowed orange, Crook sat back and sucked and chugged on his own Montecristo until a thick cloud of smoke billowed across the pavement café table.

"The end of a successful week of work always feels good buddy."

"So Marseille was successful?"

"Got what we needed." Simeon Crook patted the pocket of his jacket which held the Minolta camera.

"When do I get to find out what the job is?" Jimmy Dolan removed the cigar from his mouth and picked a stray tobacco strand from his lip.

Simeon Crook took a swig of his Jupiler and wiped the frothy residue from his moustache.

"Okay Jimmy. I need you to listen real carefully here. Some of this may seem complicated to you, okay?"

Dolan nodded and inhaled lightly, pushing cigar smoke from the corner of his mouth.

"On the other hand, parts of what I'm going to tell you will be more familiar to you than me. Understand?"

"Yeah I think so Crook..."

Simeon Crook waved his hand to let Dolan know that he was talking and didn't require a response.

"So...soccer, right. What you'd call football in Ireland..." This time he paused and Dolan nodded.

"You like soccer Jimmy? You root for a team?"

"Not really in Ireland but my English team is Liverpool."

"Okay, that's good, that's great! What about Leeds United?"

"Leeds? Yeah they're a good team, champions last year. They're actually in the European Cup Final next week."

Simeon Crook grinned and clapped his hands then spread them wide.

"Yes! They are Jimmy! They're going to be playing in the Euro series play off right here in Paris!"

Simeon Crook sat back in his seat and blew a cloud of cigar smoke over his shoulder towards a table of smartly dressed pensioners who coughed and spluttered theatrically. Jimmy Dolan looked over Crook's shoulder and grimaced.

"Ah fuck them Jimmy...You got a fucking problem buddy?" Crook half leant over his shoulder then waved his hand dismissively.

"So, yeah, Euro Final. Leeds United. That's the job."

Jimmy Dolan shook his head.

"You've lost me Crook, what's the job?"

"Okay, okay, so listen carefully now alright?" Crook stabbed the end of his cigar towards Dolan and leant forward over the table, lowering his voice.

"Argentina, okay? You know Argentina right?"

Dolan nodded uncertainly.

"Well, as you may know, but probably don't, the old man, Peron died last year and his wife Isabel became President. Great right? I love the women's lib, burn the bras and all that stuff, right?"

Jimmy Dolan shrugged, struggling to keep up.

"Na-ah! Wrong Jimmy! The fucking country has become a basket case, hyper-inflation, tanking GDP and political in-fighting. Who cares right? Just another South American dictatorship in chaos..."

Jimmy Dolan squinted through a cloud of cigar smoke and tried in vain to look like he understood.

"But there's hope ahead! Because Argentina is due to host the soccer world series in three years. Supporters from all over the world flooding in with suit-cases filled with dollars; infrastructure projects to build stadiums and roads, employing tens of thousands; a chance to showcase Argentina to the world. Great news right Jimmy?"

"I suppose so yeah, a world cup is a really big thing." Dolan relished the chance to finally offer an opinion on something he understood.

"Yeah, great news. Unfortunately, the European football federation, and France in particular, are starting to make disapproving noises about the state of the country. Dangerous cities, bad infrastructure, lack of good hotels and restaurants, shitty stadiums and sports fields...you get the picture? Solution...move the 1978 soccer world cup to fucking France! Those sonsabitches eh Jimmy?"

Simeon Crook drained the remainder of his Jupiler and flicked a large plug of ash onto the cobbles.

"So, our clients the Argentinians need a little help to demonstrate to the football decision makers that France isn't necessarily the solution to their problems. That staging a big game in France, the capital of France even, isn't entirely risk free. That bad things can happen, even in France..."

"Bad things? I don't like the sound of that Crook, I told you I didn't know what was in that van..."

"No, no, no, Jimmy, nothing like that. Less bad." Simeon Crook smiled reassuringly and signalled to the waiter for two more beers.

"Bad like what then?"

"Bad like...maybe a good old stadium riot! Those soccer hooligans they talk about in the press running wild, smashing up the stadium, raiding the field, bashing the cops...that type of thing. So not really bad, just high spirits!

"Yeah, it can easily happen. Tottenham fans last year in Rotterdam. That was a big old carry-on!" Jimmy Dolan nodded his head as Crook's grin grew wider.

"Exactly! The English bother boys right? And I hear this team, Leeds United, have some of the toughest rowdies in the whole roster. Those guys are gonna go fucking crazy Jimmy, let me tell you!"

"But they don't just go crazy for nothing at every game Crook. Something needs to happen first."

Simeon Crook smiled and winked and leant across the table and took hold of Jimmy Dolan's right hand with his own and squeezed hard.

"Exactly Jimmy, Exactly. Something needs to happen to rile those hooligans up real good. And that's exactly where we come in son!"

# Chapter 27

**Saturday 17 May 1975, Leeds.**

*Got em! United fans Grab Final Tickets in Paris – The great European cup ticket scramble paid off for a group of Leeds United supporters today after a 400 mile dash by land and sea to Paris. The United fans arrived in Paris aboard two 'Desperation Specials' – coaches laid on by a Leeds travel firm- and immediately joined the 1200 French and British fans queuing outside the Parc des Princes stadium hoping to secure one of the remaining 10,000 match tickets which were due to go on sale at 9am.*

Alan Connolly had known. Known as soon as he saw the mid-twenties suedehead with the half-mast jeans, rip-off docs and a too-tight denim jacket leaning on the bar in the Three Legs. Known as he'd watched the lad take forty minutes to drink a half. Known as he'd moved his lips unconvincingly to the third line of 'Bertie Mee said to Don Revie'.

He'd then doubted his initial judgement as he and the lads had made their way up the Headrow, and he'd turned quickly to find that the man with the five year old Skinhead fashions wasn't following. Again, as they'd got half way down Albion Street and he'd pretended to look in Cecil Gee's window and the reflection showed no double-denim shadow ducking into the doorway of Barclay's Bank. He's a d*efinite shifty fucker brother. Something not right about him. Keep your wits about you.*

Then in the Prince of Wales, he knew for sure. There was no doubt remaining when the Suedehead pushed open the door before Alan had taken the froth off his beer, and looked straight into his eyes. *Schoolboy error there. Blown his cover straight off. Undercover? Fucking shite!*

The suedehead looked away and seemed to panic as Alan glared at him from across the bar. He muttered an order to the barmaid and turned to look at the door.

Alan nodded to attract the attention of a youth collecting glasses.

"There's no back way out of here is there?"

"Not unless you're Spiderman. Why?" The youth smiled across the bar.

Alan took a large gulp of his Tetley's and turned to Dennis Copley.

"You might need to run the bus to Paris mate."

"Eh? Why, what's up?"

Alan placed his half full glass on the bar and began to push through the early Saturday evening drinkers. The Suedehead spotted him out of the corner of his eye and headed towards the door, still holding his drink and fumbling in the inside pocket of his Brutus jacket. Once out onto Mill Hill he placed the beer glass on the roof of an Austin Allegro and held a radio transmitter to his ear as he walked quickly across the road towards the Black Lion.

Alan heard the words 'situation compromised' as he exited the pub, and before he'd got across the road the squeal of tyres on tarmac announced the arrival of a black Rover P6 turning left on two wheels from Boar Lane.

The suedehead turned to face him, his face flushed, panic in his eyes.

"Police. Stay where you are!" He pointed the handheld radio at Alan, who smiled back at him.

"That's not a gun son. You can't shoot me with that you know."

The Rover screeched to a halt in the middle of Mill Hill and two men in suits were already out of the doors by the time Alan turned to face them.

"Armed police. Get on the floor, on your stomach." Alan turned back towards the pub, from where the LS9 Asylum lads were spilling onto the pavement, as a blue police van, siren wailing and lights flashing, arrived against the traffic flow on Bishopgate Street.

"Alan, spread your arms and get on the floor now. You're under arrest." The first man from the car advanced slowly towards him and the suedehead approached from the front.

"He HAS got a gun Alan. Do what he says."

"For fuck's sake, this is a new suit." Alan announced loudly and the lads in the pub doorway laughed as he slowly prostrated himself on the road outside the Black Lion.

"I'll get Ambler down Alan. Don't worry, he'll have you out in time for 'final!" Dennis Copley shouted from the doorway as Alan was pushed into the back of the car.

The suedehead laughed as he got in alongside him.

"I wouldn't bank on that....Unless Leeds are going to be in the European Cup final in the year 2000."

# Chapter 28

**Saturday 17 May 1975, Paris.**

"26...27...28. Only two away from thirty, which was the target!" Simeon Crook patted a pile of blue tickets resting on the table of the café on Rue Véron.

Jimmy Dolan half-heartedly peeled the top ticket from the pile.

"Finale de la Coupe des Clubs Champions Europeens. Tribue Presidentielle. 70 Francs. How much did you pay for them?"

"I offered the Lycee kids 100 per ticket. They could buy three each today so they made 90 francs each for a couple of hours queuing. The ticket scalpers will be asking at least 500."

"So you'll make a killing." Jimmy Dolan nodded in admiration but Simeon Crook was already shaking his head.

"No, no, no Brendan. That's not the plan..."

"It's not?"

"No buddy, no. This is our way in with the hooligans. Sure, I'll be looking to make a little, but this isn't about scalping. We'll undercut the gougers and that will endear us to the Bother Boys." Crook grinned at the ingenuity of his own plan and pushed his shades onto the top of his head.

"Well, I don't want to burst your bubble, but you might not have needed the tickets." Dolan took a swig of his drink and drummed his fingers on the table.

"Why buddy, what's the matter?"

"Gerry came round today, you know, the guy who brings the cash? Brought me a message, so he did."

"Yeah? Bad news?" Crook removed the shades from his head and rubbed them on the sleeve of his shirt.

"I don't know. A month ago I'd have said it was good news, but now I'm not sure..."

Simon Crook shrugged and spread his palms, inviting Dolan to elaborate.

"They've sent for me Crook. Said I have to go home."

Simeon Crook's mouth fell open and his lips moved as if to speak, but he remained silent and instead took a swig of his beer.

"They're bringing me back over on a bus full of Leeds fans. Bunch of nutcases too by all accounts. They say the passports won't be getting checked at Calais or Dover. Then I'll be picked up in Kent and taken to a safe house in England. I'll be back home in a couple of weeks."

Simeon Crook remained silent, his eyes blinking rapidly, the beer froth remaining on his moustache.

"What are you thinking? Do you think it's good news or not?" Jimmy Dolan shuffled in his seat as he tried to interpret Crook's reaction.

"I think...it's bad news. Very bad news for you Brendan. But it's also an opportunity. Come, let's walk."

Simeon Crook stood up quickly and produced two 10 franc notes which he stuffed under the ashtray.

"But, we haven't finished our drinks..." Jimmy Dolan was left talking to no one as he swilled down his beer and took a swig from Crook's glass before jogging to catch him up.

"I need to walk to think. Give me a minute." Crook held up his hand as they headed along Rue Artistide. As they approached the T-junction at Rue des Abbesses he stopped abruptly and turned to Dolan who was trailing in his wake.

"Okay Brendan. Here's how I see it." He paused as a black woman in a colourful turban edged past them on the footpath. "They want you back there to get rid of you, that's pretty obvious. However, this football hooligan angle is interesting."

Jimmy Dolan shook his head and sat down on a low wall.

"What...so...you really think they're going to top me?"

"I'm certain of it Brendan, yes. You're a loose end. A risk. Just like I am to the CIA." Crook rested his hand on Dolan's shoulder.

"They'll most likely have your grave already prepared somewhere near the pick-up point. Within half an hour of getting off that bus..." Crook formed a pistol shape with his fingers and levelled it at Dolan's temple. "Pow!"

"Ah fucking hell, no." Jimmy Dolan looked up at Crook and a tear welled in his left eye then spilled slowly down his cheek.

"I'm afraid so son. Just clearing out the stable again, and unfortunately you're the horseshit this time."

"So I need to run...get away now, before they come for me." Dolan stood up and wiped at his eye. "And you can help me get away, live under the radar like you do."

"Yeah, yeah, okay Jimmy. But let's not be hasty now, we gotta think about this. How we can use this situation to our advantage right?"

"I suppose so, yeah....but how?"

Simeon Crook took a firm grip of Dolan's shoulders and looked into his tear-filled eyes.

"We don't have to go seeking out any Leeds hooligans now. They'll be coming straight to us. And when they do, we have something they want." Crook produced the handful of tickets from his pocket and waved it under Dolan's nose.

"Then we'll show them Paris, a real Crook and Brendan night out, then watch the soccer final, which I promise will be a night no one will ever forget. And when they wake up in the morning, we'll already be gone. It's perfect Brendan, fucking perfect son!"

# Chapter 29

**Sunday 18 May 1975, Leeds.**

*Fairy Godmother Jim! – Boxing champ Joe Bugner is facing the most entertaining fight of his life...against an attractive young woman! The fight is being set up by Jimmy Savile for a new TV show in which he plays 'fairy godmother' to grant wishes for viewers. Other stunts planned are a schoolboy who wants to play for Manchester United, a boy who wants to slide down a fireman's pole and two girls who want to rob a bank. 'There are plenty more crazy scenes to come' promised Jimmy about his new show which starts on May 31.*

"Morning Alan. Sleep well?"

Alan Connolly lifted his head from a small wooden table in a windowless interview room within the gothic bowels of Millgarth Police station, and observed the two men in suits who entered through a creaking steel door.

"What time is it?" Connolly rubbed at his eyes as the first man scraped a chair across the tiled floor and sat down, ignoring his question.

"Where's my solicitor?"

The second man placed a heavy manila folder on the table with a thud, then removed his jacket and carefully hung it on the chair back. He then unfastened his top button and loosened his tie and sat down, fixing Alan with a squinting glare which caused him to smirk.

Both men were in their mid-forties with clothes two decades older, and thinning, brylcreamed hair. One had a top lip which bore a thick scar from a hare lip or an old wound which caused a permanent sneering uplift. Their sallow complexions and expanded waistlines spoke of days spent in darkened offices, evenings in even darker pubs, and nights sleeping in foul smelling, stake-out cars.

"This place doesn't get any better does it? There was shit dripping through the ceiling in my cell." Alan Connolly sniffed and looked up at a brown stain circling a bare bulb in the ceiling.

"It's closing down next year. They're building a new nick on the same spot. Should be ready in a couple of years. Something to look forward to when you eventually get out." Scarface sneered a twisted smile.

Alan smiled. "Where's my solicitor?"

The silent, jacketless man opened the file and his scar-faced colleague held out his hand and was passed a piece of typed paper.

"Prevention of Terrorism Act 1974. Section 7.2. You can be held for 72 hours without charge or access to legal advice. That can be extended to 5 days by authorisation of the Home Secretary." The man held the sheet up briefly then passed it back to his colleague.

"And?" Alan folded his arms and shrugged.

"And what?" The man breathed loudly through his nose and his twisted upper lip twitched slightly.

"What's Prevention of Terrorism got to do with me?"

"DETFAC." The jacketless man spoke with a sharp Northern Irish accent as he glanced up briefly from shuffling the sheaf of papers in the file.

"You've lost me..."

"DETFAC. Weapons and Ordnance. Date Expired, Test Failed and Confiscated. Processed by the Royal Engineers Logistics Corps at Catterick and sent for disposal in landfill. Or to put it in terms you'll understand, dodgy guns and ammo that were meant to be destroyed but have somehow found their way into an arms cache in County Antrim."

Both men now fell silent and stared across the table. *You know the score brother. Don't blink. Don't lick your lips. Don't swallow. Wait a few seconds before answering.*

"I'm sorry gents, I've not got a clue what you're talking about."

Before Alan had finished speaking, the Irishman had retrieved a typed sheet of paper from the file and placed it on the table in front of him.

"See that number?"

Alan glanced down to see 0532 621582 in red print. He shrugged.

"That's your number. Registered to Rita Bernard at Lascelles Terrace. Your address." The man with the scar was doing the talking and Alan sensed the weight of the Irishman's stare, sizing him up.

"That number was called on April 23rd from a number in Catterick registered to Malcolm Routledge, a farmer and landfill site operator. Mr. Routledge had been arrested earlier that day. How do you explain that call?"

"No idea pal. Maybe a wrong number?" Alan struggled to suppress a smile. *Fuck me brother, if that's all they've got it looks like your old farmer has kept his mouth shut after all.*

"Mr. Routledge is still in custody facing serious charges. How old do you think he is Alan?"

Alan Connolly began to laugh. "How would I know how old he is, I've never heard of the bloke."

"He's sixty eight. On remand in Armley and not doing too well by all accounts. How do you think he's going to react when he realises he's going down for 25 years? That he'll die in there? When we offer a deal to come up with a name, do you really think he'll keep his mouth shut Alan?"

Both men fell silent again, both with arms folded, expressions deadpan, staring across the table at him.

"As I said, I don't know the bloke, so I couldn't comment." *They're right though brother. He's got nothing to lose. Die in the nick or grass you up and get a new life in protective custody. Easy decision.*

The man with the scar snorted back a globule of phlegm into his throat and swallowed it noisily, then undid his top button and shook his tie loose. The Irishman shook his head slightly and tapped on a notepad with a biro.

"We've got all day Alan. In fact we've got three days, five if we need them. It'll be a lot easier for all of us though if you just tell us what you know. Who your Irish contact is." The man across the desk yawned and looked at his watch. Alan watched as the Irishman began to doodle on the blank page of his notepad. A square enclosed by a bigger square, then another and another.

"How old are you Alan?"

Alan Connolly shrugged. "Don't really count birthdays."

"Twenty eight." The Irishman glanced at a sheet on top of the file then resumed his doodling, a series of concentric circles now forming alongside the kaleidoscopic square.

"Twenty eight...how many years have you spent in jail since you were sixteen Alan?" The scar flashing a harsh white above dry grey lips.

"Ask your mate." Alan put his hands on the table and leant forward smiling.

The Irishman sighed loudly and broke off from inking a dark triangle onto his notepad to run a finger down the sheet of paper in the file. He puffed out his cheeks and laughed quietly.

"It's easier to count how many years he hasn't been locked up."

"How many?" The slick-haired, scar-faced man regarded Alan with undisguised contempt as the Irishman slowly extended the fingers on his right hand one at a time, stopping at four.

"He's been out five years in total in his adult life, if that." The Irishman resumed his doodling, the black triangle now extending to take the form of a bird's wing, leaving his colleague to pick up the conversation.

"Do you know what that tells me Alan?"

Alan Connolly sat back in the chair and raised his eyebrows.

"It tells me that you're a career criminal, but also that you're not a very good one. You've spent more time inside than out. That's not a successful career by anyone's reckoning."

Alan Connolly tightened his lips to ensure his smile didn't slip, as his brother's laughter echoed in his mind. *Ha Ha, they've got a point there brother, you can't deny it.*

"And now this. You've spent most of your teens and twenties in a cell, and now you'll be spending every single day of your thirties and most of your forties locked up too. You'll be a middle aged man when you get out." The sneer turned into a satisfied smile as the man glanced down at his colleague's pad which now displayed the thick black wing of a raven below the squares and circles.

The man with the scar looked at Alan who stared back across the table, the only sound the scratch of the Irishman's biro on his pad.

"And then there's your brother...Keith."

"What about him?" *Here we go brother, here we fucking go.*

"Terrible thing that happened to him. Tortured wasn't it?" The man glanced towards his colleague who tutted and put down his pen to flick through the papers in the manila folder and pass across a typed sheet.

"Oh dear.... ears and fingers cut off with shears. Teeth extracted with pliers. And you were there?" The scar-faced man lowered the paper and regarded Alan with mock concern.

Alan Connolly shook his head, the smile now vanished. *That's harsh brother. You were only there at the end. It was already ankle deep in fucking teeth by the time you arrived.*

"Oh and look at this..." Scarface shook his head and looked at Alan over the top of the A4 sheet.

"Poor Keith then took his own life while a patient at Rampton Hospital. How tragic! How must you feel about that Alan?"

Alan Connolly sank his nails into the flesh of his left arm beneath the table and stared at two black raven's wings on the notepad as the electricity crackled in his brain.

"How must you feel, knowing your brother was slowly taken apart by those animals, then killed himself in a mental ward... and it was all your fucking fault?"

"It's not working pal." Alan stared back across the table, unflinching despite the white noise buzzing in his head. "Do you know how many times I've sat in a room like this with cunts like you? You're not even any good at it. I know what comes next too. The dark room, cold room, wet room, the dungeons of Millgarth. Then sleep deprivation, food and water deprivation, lights on at night, lights off in the day, music all night...you got any Stones by the way?" Alan grinned but his mouth felt dry and he could feel a vein pulsing in his temple.

The frozen sneer remained across the table, but the man's eyes narrowed and his nostrils flared slightly as the realisation dawned that this would be as tough as they'd feared.

Again the only sound in the room was the scratch of the biro nib on the notepad, as the Irishman slouched in his chair and added a larger triangle between the two black wings. Eventually the man with the scar stood up, scraping his chair over the tiles and stooped to whisper to his partner, loud enough for Alan to hear.

"Fuck this. Let's just let them have him."

"Aye. Happy with that. Fucking waste of time." The Irishman didn't look up from his pad as his colleague left the room.

Alan Connolly licked at his cracked lips and felt his tongue, dry and heavy, sticking to the roof of his mouth.

"Can I get some water?"

The Irishman ignored him and continued filling in the dark body of the bird, its wings spread wide on either side.

"I guess that's a no then." *This is just the start brother, you know how it goes.*

After ten minutes, the Irishman's head began to sag towards his chest and his eyelids slowly lowered. The biro twitched gently in his hand, and the only sound now was the clanking and growling of Millgarth's ancient plumbing system. *I know what you're thinking brother, take the cunt hostage, hold the pen to his throat. Forget it, they'll never let you walk out of here alive.*

After another twenty minutes the metal door opened with a bang and the Irishman sat upright with a start as his colleague re-appeared.

"No fucker there. They're all out on a job."

He pulled out the chair and sat down and stared across the table.

"Do you believe in fate Alan?"

Alan Connolly shrugged.

"Because I just went to hand you over to Leeds CID, but there was no one there. And that makes me wonder whether someone up there, some greater power maybe, is looking after you, giving you another chance. Because believe me, the local coppers here fucking hate you with a passion, and they've got a list of charges as long as your arm to bring down on you."

The scar-faced man held out his right hand and without looking up, the Irishman passed him a printed sheet.

"Drug possession with intent to supply, malicious wounding, possession of an illegal firearm, discharge of an illegal firearm in a public place, possession of an offensive weapon, criminal damage, fraud, affray...my oh my, you've been a busy boy haven't you Alan?"

Alan Connolly held his breath to try to slow his heart beat, and shuffled his feet as a deep feeling of doom began to form in the pit of his stomach. *Fuck me brother, they know everything. That fat black bastard has done a proper job on you.*

The sheet of paper was handed back to the Irishman who placed it back in the file, then continued to add a circle surrounded with swirls above the body of the black ink bird on his notepad.

"You see Alan...we were your only chance. Your best option. We have the ability to do a deal. Leeds police don't give a fuck about national security or the bigger picture. They're just small-time local plod wanting to put one over on a minor criminal like you. And believe me, they really will put one over on you with that list. Concurrent sentences, what do you think he's looking at Tommy?"

The Irishman didn't look up, now adding wide, staring eyes and a downcast mouth to a human face on top of the bird's black body and wings.

"Twenty. Easy."

"Yeah, I'd say around that. So again Alan, you're spending all your thirties locked up again. What a fucking waste of a life eh?" The man with the scar placed both elbows on the table and clenched his fists beneath his chin.

Alan Connolly closed his eyes and breathed deeply through his nostrils, feeling his chest rise and fall as his stomach did back-flips. *Be careful brother. Don't let them stitch you up.*

"Let's say I did know something and I provided the information you need. What's the deal? What would I be looking at?" The scar-faced man's face remained impassive, but his knuckles whitened beneath his chin and the Irishman stopped scratching at his pad and raised his eyes.

"It would depend what you gave us, who we nick, how important they are in the command structure."

Alan Connolly nodded and took a deep breath.

"I'm not saying I know this stuff, but speaking..."

"Hypothetically? Give us an example of what some imaginary person might know and I'll give you an idea of what we might be able to arrange."

"This is off the record right?"

"Do you see a tape recorder? We're fucking Special Branch pal, we work strictly off the record." The Irishman was sitting up now, his pen tapping on his notepad.

"M62 Coach bombing." He'd said it now. The bare bulb flickered and the electrical current surged through the room as the two men at the other side of the table tried and failed to hide their interest.

"What about it?"

"The man who transported the bomb. What if someone knew where he was?"

The man with the scar licked at his lips and the two men glanced at each other, as if deciding who should speak.

"If you delivered him, we could make all the other charges go away, I'm confident of that." The Irishman didn't hesitate.

"What, so all the Leeds CID charges and the landfill stuff?"

The man with the scar seemed unsure and half turned towards his colleague, but the Irishman didn't blink.

"If you deliver him, we can definitely clear the Leeds stuff. The DETFAC offence is terror related, harder to lose, so we'd need more than just him."

Alan Connolly nodded. "What if I could deliver the M62 man and the contacts who are looking after him?"

The Irishman's eyes flashed and he swallowed hard causing his Adam's Apple to bulge in his throat.

"Him and those shielding him? Yes, we could do that."

"All charges dropped?"

The Irishman nodded. "When?"

"Before the end of the month."

The Irishman turned slowly to the man with the scar.

"Go make the call."

Scarface stood, his flushed face highlighting the white scar stretching from his upper lip to his nose. He paused as if to speak then hurried from the room.

The Irishman picked up his biro and began chewing the end. "I need to make sure you aren't bullshitting us Alan."

"What would be the point?"

"I just need to check. We already know the identity of the man who transported the bomb. I'm going to read you a list of names. When you hear me say his name, let me know."

Alan Connolly nodded.

"Abbott, O'Brien..." *Still time to back out brother...*

"Callaghan, Derry..." *I hope you've got a plan. The provos will track you down wherever they put you...*

"Dolan..." The Irishman didn't take his eyes from the notepad.

"Jimmy. Jimmy Dolan. He's your boy." Alan Connolly's words came out as a whisper and now the Irishman was looking up from his notepad, his notepad with the black wings and black body and wide, crying eyes and upturned smile of an angel.

"Fuck me Alan. What have you got yourself into?" The Irishman's eyes as wide and dark as his angel's. The door opened with a bang and the man with the scar entered, his face flushed red, eyes blinking fast.

"I made the call. It's on. Alan, you've got a deal."

# Chapter 30

**Monday 19 May 1975, Leeds.**

***Big Match ticket probe****- Leeds United have promised an investigation into the problem of European Cup final ticket touts and said that they will try to trace the origin of any black markets tickets recovered by police. General Manager Mr Keith Archer has said that any fan proved to be selling tickets on the black market would be banned. Investigations have started into deals where touts and agencies were asking more than £100 for tickets. Mr Archer said that Leeds have claimed 100 £13 tickets for the final for the directors, players' wives, officials and staff in the official party. The players each received 'a handful' but he declined to be more specific about the number.*

"Did you sleep better last night Alan? I know it's not the Dragonara but we asked for you to be put in a better cell. Do you take sugar?" The Irishman produced a handful of white sachets from his jacket pocket.

"Why am I still here?" Alan Connolly paced back and forth across the tiled floor of the interview room.

"I told you, paperwork. We need the Home Secretary's sign off on things at this level. I'm sorry. Hopefully by lunchtime."

"What have Leeds CID said?"

"They don't know what's going on and we'll keep it that way. You'll be released under investigation, charges pending, details restricted under the Official Secrets Act, Prevention of Terrorism Act and all the rest of it.

Basically they'll be told to keep their fucking Yorkshire noses out."

"And definitely no one is going to break rank and lift Dolan in France when I meet him?" Alan continued to pace, his mind filled with dark thoughts and conspiracy theories.

"There's no appetite for that high up. We'd be caught up in red tape trying to extradite him for the next two years."

"And you're 100% sure the arrest will go down exactly as we've agreed?"

"You have my word Alan. It will be dressed up as a routine customs check at Dover, and you and some of your lads will get lifted too."

Alan Connolly nodded and bit his lip and rubbed the sweat from his palms onto the front of his trousers.

"A few of the lads will be tooled up. I'll definitely be carrying too, so make it look good."

"Your famous bayonet is making the trip to Paris then?"

Alan Connolly smiled. "Aye. It's a family heirloom too, so I want it back."

"I'll see what I can do." The Irishman blew on a paper cup of coffee. "If this comes off Alan, it's a big thing. A really big thing. You'll be helping to put some bad people away. People who kill kids."

Alan Connolly looked down at his feet and sipped at his tea.

"But make no mistake. If this goes wrong, it's going to be a fucking disaster for all of us. If Dolan isn't on that bus when it gets stopped at Dover, there's absolutely nothing I can do to lose those charges. You'll cop for the whole lot. Understand?"

Alan Connolly nodded and pressed his back against the interview room wall to try and stop his whole body shaking, as a thousand volts pulsed and crackled in his brain. Then above the electrical white noise came the usual sound of his brother's mocking tones. *Let's just hope wee Jimmy plays nice for you brother. Because if he decides not to come home you won't have to worry about this lot, the fucking IRA will kill you before you've even got out of Kent.*

# Chapter 31

**Sunday 25 May 1975, Paris.**

Jimmy Dolan blinked through streaming, stinging eyes, trying to focus on the white shapes on a brown wall where pictures had once hung. He coughed and inhaled deeply through a wet towel held over his nose and mouth.

"Go out for a walk Jimmy. I told you, you don't need to be in here." Simeon Crook's voice was muffled beneath a surgical mask, and he blinked through condensation droplets on the lenses of a pair of motorcycle goggles and stirred a steaming pan on the stove of the attic flat in Pigalle.

"How long is it going to take?" Dolan choked through the towel and closed his eyes tight.

"Half an hour maybe. It has to be cooked into crystals."

"It feels like fucking poison, so it does." Dolan pulled the towel over his face and swallowed vinegar saliva.

"Well, essentially that's what it is buddy. If you don't get the mix right, it will kill you straight off. Sometimes that's what we want, but this time, we need to get it just right. Something to keep those English guys partying real hard all night."

"And you can buy all that stuff from the pharmacy here? That's pure madness. Would never happen back home."

Crook turned, a wooden spatula emitting chemical steam in his hand. "Oh it would son. Field chemistry. One of the most useful things the company taught me. With the right combination of over-the-counter ingredients, you can create anything from a bomb to a lethal poison to the ultimate party drug."

"I can't wait to learn all this stuff." Jimmy Dolan coughed into the towel.

"You betcha buddy!"

A knock at the flat door caused both men to turn, then exchange panicked glances.

"Who is it?" Crook slowly opened the kitchen drawer and withdrew a large bread knife.

"Livrer du Boucher Marcel." A man's voice echoed off the bare walls of the landing.

"Shit. That isn't meant to be here until tomorrow." Simeon Crook approached the door but didn't open it and lowered the mask to speak.

"Merci monsieur. Laisse-le devant la porte." Blinking behind the goggles he pushed his ear to the door, then waited until he'd heard the sound of heavy footsteps on the wooden stairs and the slam of the front door, before sliding back the bolt. He stooped to pick up a square cardboard box wrapped in brown tape from the wooden floor.

"Ah shit. Fuck. It's leaking." Crook carried the box into the room and placed it on the floor then stared down at his wet palms. "Brendan, I need you to go get some ice."

Crook pulled up his mask and returned to stirring the toxic mix on the stove as Dolan approached blinking through raw, red eyes.

"Ice? How much?"

"As much as you can carry. Enough to fill that refrigerator." Crook nodded to a rust coated white cabinet in the corner of the room. "And be quick buddy, that thing is melting fast."

"What is it?"

"Never mind that son. Just go get that ice. And bring a bottle of brandy too. I'll need a drink after cooking this shit up."

# Chapter 32

**Monday 26 May 1975, Leeds.**

*Fans in Hotel Fight- Members of a coach party of Scotsmen on their way to Wembley for Saturday's Home International soccer clash between England and Scotland were involved in a fight in a Warrington hotel on Friday night. Five of them were hurt and taken to hospital. The incident occurred at the Longford Hotel where the Scotsmen were involved in clashes with local youths. In Wembley, several hundred fans invaded the London Esso Hotel near the ground early on Saturday, but the management allowed 200 to stretch out on the deep-pile carpet until the bar opened at 10.30am.*

"What time's 'bus coming Alan?" Terry Jackson approached the bar of the Waterloo pub, his hands twisted into tattooed claws clutching ten empty pint glasses.

"Meant to be here at seven. Why? Had enough of this lot already?" Alan Connolly smiled as he surveyed the chaos of the tap room.

The older lads, Dennis Copley, Market Dave, Fat Lawrence, Franks Meadows and the Macleod brothers were sat surrounded by empty pint glasses, beneath a large Union Jack bearing a grinning skull and cross bones with the legend Leeds United- LS9 Asylum. They raised their arms and yelled their encouragement as young Geoff swayed precariously on a table and led the younger lads in a chorus of 'I was born under the Gelderd End.' Around the bar and seated at scattered tables piled with empty glasses were assembled the other thirty or so passengers who'd paid £16 to secure a place on the Asylum's trip to Paris for the European Cup Final.

In the corner of the room, at a table next to the one armed bandit where Non-Stop Nigel robotically yanked at the arm, Steve exchanged a glance with Alan and shook his head. Assigned to babysit Eugene Wilson, after half an hour he was already tiring of the legendary Seacroft jailbird's tales. At the other side of the bar, Norman Cowell and Brian Scott reminisced about music and scooters, pills and dance halls and past finals spent in prison.

"What time boat are we on then?" Fat Lawrence, wearing a brown double-breasted 'Shaft' trench-coat, shouted down the bar.

"4am ferry. We should be in Paris mid-morning." Alan curled his top lip as he swigged off a tumbler of the Waterloo's finest rip-off Scotch.

"We'll get some scran, batter some touts then we can look for a bar that stays open all night. Sorted for two days then!" Tommy Mcleod had his Paris agenda sorted out.

*'Knives are made for stabbing, guns are made to shoot. If you come in the Gelderd End we'll put in the boot.'* Geoff sloshed beer from his half-full pint onto the table and struggled to maintain his balance in three inch platform soles. He then produced a yellow woollen hat with blue and white stripes from his jacket pocket and pulled it over his head, balaclava style. The other lads cheered and broke into a deafening rendition of 'Gelderd aggro' with some producing balaclavas of their own, complete with eye and mouth holes cut into the wool.

"Who the fuck made them?" Fat Lawrence laughed and shook his head.

"Geoff's sister is a seamstress at Hepworth's. She ran them a dozen off." Terry Jackson shook his head as he returned with another double handful of empties.

Dennis Copley swayed across the room and joined Alan at the bar.

"Time for another Al?"

Connolly glanced at a cracked plastic clockface on the wall behind the bar.

"Aye. If the bus comes early they'll let you take it on anyway. It's Blind Eddie driving. He won't give a fuck. We've got a few crates from Davenports and about ten Party 7's for the journey down too."

"Same again Terry, and whatever the main man here is having."

The two men leant on the bar and watched as the whole room began banging ashtrays and pint glasses on the tables, as Geoff stamped his feet on the table and the pub reverberated to a deafening refrain of 'We're gonna win the European Cup.'

"You can't beat this can you Al? European Cup Final. I just hope it hasn't come too late."

"What do you mean?"

"Well, Revie has gone and this team isn't going to go on forever. Big Jack's packed in. Gilesy is looking at going into management. Billy's 33. Norman's 32. Look at this season, not even qualifying for Europe if we don't win on Wednesday. Last season, I'd have been confident against Munich. This year, not as much."

Alan Connolly placed his hand on Copley's shoulder.

"Well, whatever happens mate, we'll have a good few days. Make the most of it."

"Too right Alan, you need to enjoy times like these, big European finals. You never know when you'll get to do it again."

Alan Connolly took a swig of his drink as he spotted the dark shadow of a 40-seater coach appear through the half-frosted glass of the tap room window.

"Very true Dennis. Enjoy it. None of us might be around next time we get there." Alan Connolly threw back his drink.

"Come on Asylum! Drink up. Paris here we come!"

## Chapter 33

**Tuesday 27 May 1975, Paris.**

*Mass Exodus- And 'Hope' is the password. The great exodus of Leeds United fans to Paris began today, and the password for all on the journey was HOPE. Hope that some last tickets for the European cup final will still be on sale. Hope that touts might turn a kindly face and cut their asking price for tickets. And hope, most of all, that Leeds' long trek to this match will end with the team finally delivering the European cup to Elland Road.*

Jimmy Dolan knelt on the tiled floor of the Pigalle bedsit attic in his underpants, his legs splayed out behind him like a frog. He tilted his head and looked into the black, unseeing eyes staring back at him, their long white eyelashes frosted with ice. Thick yellow whiskers protruded from a snow-coated snout and Dolan couldn't resist slowly extending his hand to feel their spikey bristles.

"Shit Brendan, what are you doing man? Close the door or the ice will melt." Simeon Crook entered the room in his going out clothes- a floral paisley shirt with a spear collar and a tan leather safari jacket.

"Why a pig's head though Crook? A sheep head would have fit in the ice compartment. Easier to carry too."

"I told you. The referee is a Jew. A sheep is a ruminant, it chews cud and has split hooves, so that's fine and dandy for your Jew to handle and eat. It's called Kosher. Swine isn't Kosher. Pig is forbidden for the Jew. A Jew will freak out at a pig's head. So a pig's head it is for Monsieur Saloman."

"But you said he already knows what he has to do. Why do we need this too?" Jimmy Dolan hauled himself upright as Crook unwrapped a large plastic sheet and placed it on the floor.

"Just a reminder. It's nearly two weeks since I went to Marseille. Two weeks since I met him outside his office and showed him the photos of his wife picking up the kids from school, his old mother at the supermarche. Told him what he needs to do to keep them safe. I need to make sure that he knows we're serious. That we're here in Paris and we can get to him whenever we want." Crook nodded at the bottom shelf of the fridge then at the plastic sheet, and Jimmy Dolan screwed up his face as he stooped to pick up the pig's head with both arms and slowly lower it onto the sheet.

"Okay, put some ice on it now then wrap it good and tight." Crook retrieved a square cardboard box from the corner of the room and placed it on the formica topped table. "What time are the Brits arriving?"

"Not sure. Gerry knows we've got some match tickets so when they make contact he's going to let them know and arrange the meeting." Jimmy Dolan scooped a handful of ice from the bottom of the fridge and sprinkled it over the severed swine's head then wrapped the plastic around it. "Jesus, I hope they don't find out about this."

"Whaddaya mean Brendan?" Simeon Crook held the box open and motioned with his eyes for Jimmy to place the head inside it. "We want them to know! That's the whole point!"

Jimmy Dolan gently placed the head in the box and stepped back as Crook picked up a pair of kitchen scissors and a roll of tape.

"What? You're going to tell them? Why Crook? They'll fucking kill us."

"No they won't...we won't tell them the full story. Just that we know the referee is on the take and he's going to make sure Leeds don't win the game. Anyway, they aren't going to hurt us. We'll have provided tickets for the Euro World Series and shown them a wild time in Paris. They'll love us. That two-bit, cheating French hustler though, man, they're going to be out for that motherfucker's blood. And that's exactly what we want!" Crook closed the box and taped the lid shut, then produced a thick felt-tipped pen and began to write on the lid as Dolan craned his neck to see over his shoulder.

"Monsieur Michel Saloman c/o Hotel Napoleon. Avenue de Friedland."

"Yeah, he'll be arriving this afternoon. We need this to be waiting for him at the check-in desk when he gets there."

"So we're not posting it? We're delivering it by hand?"

"No Brendan. WE aren't delivering it by hand. You are! Go get a hat and take my shades. Straight in, don't speak, just hand it over to the desk clerk and get the hell out."

"But Crook..."

"No 'buts' Brendan. Go. Hurry. Check-in is from twelve so it needs to be delivered before then. Oh, almost forgot..."

Simeon Crook picked up the pen and leant over the box again as Jimmy Dolan slowly attempted to phonetically piece together the words.

*"Bienvenue a Paris Monsieur. Soyez Prudent. Votre visiteur a Marseille.* What's it mean Crook?"

Simeon Crook III smiled. "That doesn't matter Jimmy, just take it to the hotel then get back here. We've got a busy day, and an even busier night ahead."

## Chapter 34

The thirty members of the LS9 Asylum stood beneath a sun canopy outside Le Nombril bar and stared at the growing ranks of the CRS on the opposite side of Rue Victor Masse. The French riot police, in their black overalls and round black helmets with a small silver crest, tapped their batons on the palms of their gloved hands and stared back.

"Three nicked and it's not even midday yet. Pretty good going that, even by our standards." Norman smiled and swigged from a small bottle of Kronenbourg.

"I told them to wait until we'd sussed things out and what did they do...piled straight into the first touts they saw." Alan Connolly shook his head and watched a skinny black man in an Adidas tracksuit squatting beside the police ranks, clearly communicating with them. "That lad there, he was with them. I reckon the law are in on it, taking a cut."

"At this rate we won't need many tickets anyway. Everyone will be in jail by tomorrow night." Norman watched as Max and the young lads appeared from a sidestreet carrying two crates of beer.

"Fuck paying 10 Francs for a half, we've just done a supermarket over!" Geoff grinned as he began to hand out bottles to the lads outside the bar.

"Listen Norm, I've got to go see someone. I'll catch up with you later. Get everyone to go back to that bar in the square by Pigalle Metro about five and I'll see you there." Alan Connolly drained his beer and put the bottle on the table while monitoring the build-up of police across the road.

"See someone? Who do you know in Paris?"

"Just a bit of business. I'll be back, just try to keep this lot under control. Too many coppers here, get them to move in small groups and we'll meet up later."

"Fucking hell Alan, keep them under control? I don't think that lot over the road can do that with tear gas and a water cannon! What chance have I got?"

# Chapter 35

"Are you sure he's coming?" Alan Connolly looked up at a clock on the bell tower of the church in Montmartre and took a sip of his drink.

"He fucking better be. Or we'll be going to fetch him." Gerry Cleary checked his watch and narrowed his eyes as he scanned the square.

"What did you say this stuff is called? It tastes like cough mixture?"

"Pastis. You get used to it when you've been here for a while. The French love the stuff. Drink it for fucking breakfast, the dirty bastards."

"How long have you been here?"

"Four years. Had to go away quickly. They called it my retirement. It's okay, I get paid every month and don't have to do much. I'll be doing even less when I get rid of young Jimmy."

The clock chimed once as the large hand hit three and the two men fell silent.

"Fifteen minutes late..."

"It doesn't surprise me, the way he's been living. This fucking yank he's taken up with...something about him I don't like. Don't trust the cunt."

"What's he like?" Alan Connolly raised his glass to his lips then lowered it without drinking.

"You'll find out soon enough." Gerry Cleary nodded across the square and Alan Connolly turned his head to observe the two figures approaching from an alley on the right.

The taller man was middle aged, with a droopy moustache and grey-flecked, collar-length hair pulled into a short pony tail. He wore a paisley shirt with a wide, pointed collar, unbuttoned to mid-chest level, and a tan safari jacket. The furtive, scanned assessment of the square, the cigarette concealed between four fingers and thumb, and the quick, shuffling gait all appeared instantly familiar to Alan Connolly from Barlinnie and Armley.

The other man was younger, shorter and visibly nervous. He wore 24 inch flared jeans and matching denim jacket and a T-shirt with a Pepsi Cola logo. His flushed complexion, wide eyes and wavy light brown hair suggested a rural tourist experiencing the delights of a big city for the first time.

Gerry Cleary straightened in his seat and tilted his head slightly, raising his glass as he caught the eye of the younger man.

"Nice of you to turn up Jimmy." Gerry Cleary sniffed loudly and pushed out a chair from beneath the table with his foot.

"Are we late? Sorry Gerry, I don't have a watch."

Jimmy Dolan sat down and his older companion remained standing behind him.

"This is Alan, Jimmy." Gerry Cleary turned to Alan Connolly who extended his hand in greeting.

"Alan's the man with the bus. He's come to take you home son."

## Chapter 36

Simeon Crook III sensed Jimmy Dolan flinch as the elderly Irishman mentioned going home, and placed a reassuring hand on the shoulder of his young friend. He looked down into the eyes of the man sat across the table who now rose slightly to shake Jimmy's hand. Late twenties, dark hair with a hint of a curl, framing an angular face with a half-smile that he couldn't quite interpret.

"You're from Leeds." Crook spoke and the man looked up, dark eyes flashing, confident and challenging.

"Aye, well Glasgow originally, now Leeds." The man stood and offered his hand and Simeon Crook reached out and squeezed hard as he met his stare.

"Glasgow eh? A genuine Scotsman...shucks, we sure are gonna have some fun..."

"Alan. Alan Connolly."

"Simeon Crook. Simeon Crook, the third. It's a pleasure to meet you Alan Connolly."

"Drinks boys?" Gerry Cleary stood up and reached into his jacket for his wallet. "I'll stand you a round, then I need to be away."

Jimmy Dolan shrugged and looked up at Crook.

"Sure Gerry, If you're buying! Three beers and three Hennessy VS chasers...no, cancel the cognac, let's have three Ballantine's in honour of our celtic friend here." Crook grinned and slapped Cleary on the back.

"Fucking hell." Gerry Cleary walked towards the waiter, shaking his head as he counted out a handful of notes.

"So, Alan, you're here for the soccer play off right?"

"Aye, thought we'd come a day early so we can get hold of some tickets."

Simeon Crook sat back and smiled as Gerry returned to the table to shake Jimmy's hand and stoop to whisper something in his ear.

"Well, you just met the right guy." Crook reached into his jacket pocket then removed his hand with a flourish to brandish a sheaf of blue tickets.

"Are they real?" Alan reached out and Crook handed over a ticket. "How much?"

"Just what I paid for them. 150 francs. The scalpers are asking 500."

Now it was Alan Connolly's turn to smile. "That might be what they're asking. It's not what my boys are paying."

"Have a good couple of days lads, I'll be away now." Gerry Cleary's eyes flitted nervously from Jimmy Dolan to Alan Connolly. "And good luck Alan...with the match, I mean."

The three men watched Cleary shuffle away across the square and Alan scanned the pavement tables of the cafes and bars. A middle aged man seated alone, wearing a sports jacket and trilby hat turned the pages of Le Monde. An Oriental in his thirties in a cheese-cloth shirt and faded denim jeans met Alan's gaze then quickly looked away. MI6. IRA. They were bound to be watching, monitoring the situation all the way back to Dover, trying to stay in control.

"Where are those fucking drinks?" Simeon Crook twisted in his seat and spotted the waiter disappear into the café carrying an empty tray. "I'm going to take a piss and put a rocket up this guy's ass while I'm there."

Jimmy Dolan watched him go, fidgeting with a napkin from the table then looking down at his feet.

"So Jimmy, looking forward to going home?"

"Yeah, I suppose. Be nice to see my folks again. My wee brother. It's been a long time."

Alan Connolly nodded. "Sounds like you've had a nice little holiday over here..."

"It's been more than a holiday." Jimmy Dolan seemed to surprise himself as he interjected before Alan had finished speaking. "I've learnt so much from Crook. He's taught me about things I'd never even heard of."

"Oh yeah? What's his story? Does he live here?"

Jimmy Dolan began to laugh. "His story? His life is one big story...you wouldn't believe the things he's done."

Dolan smiled and turned his head as Crook returned carrying a silver tray containing three beers and three whiskies.

"Fucking asshole, busy slicing cherries for a Cinzano. Went behind the fucking bar and fixed these myself."

Crook placed the tray on the table and handed out the drinks.

"You and your guys got a place to stay Al?"

"Yeah, clubs and knocking shops!" Alan raised his glass and Simeon Crook met it with his own.

"I've got a room that I don't use now that I stay with Jimmy here. You could put up a dozen guys in there if they don't mind sleeping on the floor."

"Yeah great. Some of the older lads will go for that. Cheers Simon."

"It's Simeon. Simeon Crook III." Crook narrowed his eyes as the flame from his zippo disappeared in a cloud of exhaled smoke.

"So whaddya wanna do Al? Some tourist stuff?"

"It's Alan. Alan Connolly. And no, I'm not bothered for churches and towers. A good drink with my mates, a Leeds win in the final, bit of a tear-up with some Jerrys then the bus home, get Jimmy back safe to his mum. That'll do for me."

"I'll drink to that." Simeon Crook raised his glass and then kicked Jimmy Dolan beneath the table, prompting him to raise his own.

"Here's to going home." Alan Connolly extended his beer and met Jimmy Dolan's flickering eyes across the table.

"To going home." Dolan's lips moved but his words were no more than a whisper.

Alan Connolly tapped the glass hard with his own, causing Dolan to flinch.

"Cheers Jimmy. Here's to safe travels... for all of us."

# Chapter 37

*'Oh mi-lads, you should have seen their faces, going down to Elland Road to see Jim Armfield's aces..'*

The staccato beat of beer bottles on table-tops accompanied the singing, and caused passing tourists to stand and stare, and the gendarmes in their flat, peaked caps to nervously finger the batons in their belts as they observed the bar from the other side of Rue de Douai in Pigalle.

"This is so cool Alan, I just love these battle songs!" Simeon Crook rattled his bottle on the bar as the elderly barman's eyes flicked from Max and Geoff swaying on a table in the doorway, to Non-Stop Nigel hoisting the pinball table on two legs to dislodge a stuck ball. "Garcon – plus de beer for everyone!"

*'All the lads and lasses there with all their smiling faces, going down to Elland Road...'*

"Great to see Brendan....Jimmy laughing again too." Crook nodded across to a table filled with bottles where Scotty held court and Jimmy Dolan grinned on the edge of a circle of half a dozen drunken smiles.

"Taken him under your wing have you?" Alan Connolly turned towards Crook to avoid eye contact with Eugene Wilson who was picking his way slowly through the tables towards the bar.

"The kid was depressed when I met him. Lonely. Sad. Just needed bringing out of his shell is all."

*'Bertie Mee said to Don Revie, have you heard of the North Bank Highbury... '*

Crook laughed and began to clap along. "These fucking songs man, amazing!"

"So this is 'bloke who's putting me up for 'night?" Crook turned at the sound of the gravelly voice and came face to purple face with Eugene Wilson.

"I 'ope it's a double bed lad?" Wilson leant in until his nose was within an inch of Crook's and the American recoiled from his breath.

"Sure there's a bed buddy, and yeah you're welcome to use it."

"Will it fit three of us in though? I'm planning to treat meself...know what I mean?" Eugene Wilson cackled with laughter and drained a glass from the tray the barman was filling with foaming glasses on the bar. "Know what I mean Alan lad?"

Wilson's throaty laugh turned into a bronchial coughing fit and he nodded at the cigarette packet at Simeon Crook's elbow. "Pass us a gasper old lad."

"He wants a cigarette." Connolly leant in towards Crook's ear.

"An American then..." Eugene Wilson inhaled and grimaced as Crook's zippo flared beneath the Gauloises. "What you doing living here with 'frogs?"

"Well...I guess you could say part vacation, part business. Business right now." Crook took a step to the side as Alan Connolly positioned himself alongside him.

"What business is it you're in Simon, Jimmy never said?" Simeon Crook licked at his lips, feeling the weight of

Connolly's stare, while maintaining eye contact with the swaying figure of Eugene Wilson.

"I'll tell you his business!" Wilson held up a finger and grinned through golden brown teeth. "He's a fucking bank robber!"

"Huh!" Crook laughed without smiling and sensed Connolly studying him, monitoring his reaction.

"What makes you say that friend...sorry, I never caught your name?"

"Eugene Wilson, best safe cracker in East Leeds. And North and West Leeds come to think of it. South though, there was this kid in Morley..."

"Funny thing to say that Gene?" Alan Connolly picked up a glass of beer from the tray on the bar and blew the froth off the top.

"Takes one to know one doesn't it? I can tell just by looking at him. His clothes. The way he moves. How he watches the room. Fucking obvious. He's a blagger. Aren't you?"

"Well...ha!" Simeon Crook shook his head and scratched at his moustache and reached for the cigarette packet.

"So are you?" Alan didn't shift his focus from Simeon Crook who tapped his cigarette on the bar before slowly raising it to his lips and flicking at the Zippo.

*'First of all there's the boss who's right behind us, he's the one who fills our hearts with pride...'*

Alan Connolly took a step to the right so he was directly in Crook's line of sight when he looked up after lighting the Gauloises, and the American shifted uneasily beneath Connolly's unblinking stare and ambiguous smirk.

Dennis Copley reeled up to the bar and threw his arms round Eugene Wilson. "Is this our beer Alan?"

"Yeah, take it and fuck off, we're talking."

*"It's a joy to us all, when Big Jack has the ball, to know that he is on our side...'*

"*There's a red headed tiger known as Billy, and he goes like a human dynamo...*I always forget 'words after this bit. What's next Dennis?" Eugene Wilson followed Copley who was carrying the tray of drinks from the bar, before turning halfway across the room to shout back over his shoulder.

"Fucking armed robber. Am I right or am I right?"

"Ha! He's certainly a character." Simeon Crook smiled and raised his glass as Wilson roared with laughter and swayed across the room.

"He's a fucking pain in the arse, but he's no mug."

"Mug?"

"Fool. He's no fool. He usually has the measure of people. So does he this time?" Alan Connolly pulled up a tall bar stool and tapped it, prompting Crook to sit down as he remained standing.

"No offence Alan, but we've only just met. All I know is that you're an IRA man, you seem a great guy but I'm hardly likely to..."

"I'm not fucking IRA!" Alan Connolly felt the switch flick and the electricity flashed and crackled in his head. *That's what they'll think though brother, what they'll say if you get caught. IRA man. Terrorist. Traitor. That's what they'll be calling you.*

"Whoa, okay buddy. Look I don't care. We're all soldiers in someone's army at the end of the day." Simeon Crook raised his hands in mock surrender.

"I'm nothing to do with the IRA. I just got into a situation where I owed them and they asked me to bring the boy back. I didn't have a choice. I just want to get him home to his family then move on and forget all about it." *That's right brother, get the child killer back to his ma.*

Simeon Crook drew on his cigarette as Max And Geoff and a handful of the young lads spilled out to the pavement tables and began directing a chant of 'you're gonna get you're fucking heads kicked in' towards the two vans of gendarmes parked across the road. Alan Connolly leant his head in towards Crook and smelt spirit and tobacco on his breath.

"So what's the story then? Are you a bank robber?"

Crook rested on the bar as he drew on the cigarette and exhaled a cloud of smoke towards the rough yellow artex of the ceiling.

"The old guy is a pretty good judge of a character I think." He smiled and Alan Connolly nodded and watched through the window of the bar as another van arrived and disgorged a dozen CRS officers in riot gear.

"And so am I. You have to be in my line of work. I think I can trust you Alan. Right?"

"Like you said. We 're all soldiers." Alan turned to face Crook who stubbed his cigarette out on the bar and flicked the butt onto the floor.

"Right...so, yeah, I worked for some bad people Alan. Powerful people, in fact, the most powerful people in the world. I won't bore you with the detail but they decided they didn't need me and my buddies anymore." Crook lit another cigarette and signalled to the barman to fill up his glass.

"You got laid off?"

Simeon Crook's smile turned into gentle laughter.

"It was a little more serious than that. It would have been more laid out than laid off, if you follow? So yeah, we had to disappear quickly. I left with nothing, a suitcase of clothes, a few thousand bucks in the bank. All the guys were in the same position. All we had were the skills the company had taught us...urban warfare, spycraft, espionage, advanced weapons skills, explosives..."

Alan Connolly's eyes widened. "Who the fuck were you working for?"

"The US Government." Crook narrowed his eyes and sucked on the Gauloises, revelling in the sudden shift in the demeanour of the previously cocky young man standing alongside him.

"So, yeah we hit a few banks in the mid-west, away from the major cities. We'd pull five, sometimes ten grand a time. Too much risk for too little reward. We needed a big score to set us up, get us out of the country and form the international RAD Team network."

"What's RAD Team?" Alan Connolly pulled up a bar stool and edged closer to Crook.

"Retired. Angry. Dangerous. All ex-CIA boys like me, who learnt that being one of the good guys leaves you financially exposed and in danger. To succeed in this life you need to be a nastier bastard than they are."

"Too right..." Alan Connolly's eyes flashed from the barstool as Crook paused, savouring the recognition.

"So what was the big job?"

Simeon Crook III took a deep breath and scanned the room then leant in towards Connolly.

"North West Airlines Flight 305."

Alan Connolly blinked as smoke from Crook's cigarette hung between them in a fine mist.

"What? What is that?"

"November '71..." Crook held the cigarette between four fingers and thumb and raised it to his lips.

"I was inside then."

"Don't you get newspapers in British prisons?"

Alan Connolly shrugged.

"DB Cooper?"

"No sorry, never heard of him."

"Jeez Alan, it was only the most audacious hijacking in the history of aviation. DB Cooper boarded a 727 in Portland with a bomb in a suitcase, had the plane flown to Seattle and asked for two hundred grand in used notes...and four parachutes."

"Fucking hell, the parachute hijacking, I do remember! That was you? Jesus fucking Christ! Everyone in Armley was talking about it for weeks. You jumped out of that plane with the bag of cash and got away with it!" Alan Connolly was off the barstool now, shaking his head as he paced back and forth alongside the bar.

"Sssshhhh!" Crook beckoned him to sit down. "I didn't do the jump, that was my buddy Edgar. He served in the 187th Airborne in Korea. I was one of the extraction team who picked him up from the forest in Washington State."

"Two hundred grand! Jumping out of a fucking jet! That has to be a contender for crime of the century..." Alan Connolly took Crook's hand and squeezed it hard.

A loud cheer caused both men to turn to see an unlit Juke Box in the corner of the room flicker into life as the old barman fiddled with the cables behind it. Norman cast his critical eye over the selection available.

"Fucking Johnny Hallyday and Serge Gainsbourg...haven't they heard of reggae in France?"

"Here Alan, there's one for you!" Norman turned and waved and a minute later Brian Jones sitar intro and Charlie Watts machine-gun drumbeat paved the way for Jagger's vocals as Paint it Black crackled from the speakers.

"So you like the Stones huh?" Crook turned towards Alan Connolly who flashed a thumbs-up in Norman's direction.

"Best band ever. I've liked them since 63. Jagger is my hero. Does what he wants, doesn't give a fuck what anyone else thinks."

"Yeah, that's the image alright. Underneath it all though he's just another scared kid."

"How would you know?"

"Listen buddy, when you've had to pick him up off the bathroom floor in a shitty motel, crying his eyes out because he thinks someone is about to take him out, then you see what's really under that tough guy façade."

"What? You've actually met Jagger?" Alan Connolly was off the barstool again, dark eyes wide, hands gripping Simeon Crook's arms.

Simeon Crook laughed and stood up, shrugging Alan's hands away.

"Too many stories buddy! This is one for later. C'mon, let's get the boys another drink and get some of those old battle songs going again."

# Chapter 38

**Wednesday 28 May 1975, Paris.**

*All the Best! Leeds United set off on their historic trip to Paris for the European Cup final against Bayern Munich with a 'good luck' message from fans at Yeadon airport yesterday. Hundreds of supporters ranging from tiny tots to pensioners lined the airport approaches as the team bus arrived with a police escort. Most of the 500 fans who had been waiting since 9am then followed the European cup finalists to the departure lounge and watched as the team boarded a Boeing 737 Aer-Lingus flight. As the plane took off the fans chanted 'we're going to win the cup.'*

"Jeez Brendan, what happened to you? Brendan... Jimmy...wake up son." Simeon Crook placed his hand on Jimmy Dolan's shoulder and shook him until he slowly lifted his head from the table of the pavement café in Place Pigalle.

"Oh...shit...what time is it?" Dolan blinked and opened one red eye then immediately closed it.

"9am. Where'd you sleep?"

"Jesus...fuck knows. I just got booted out of Les Taxi-Girls though so probably there."

"Where are the rest of the guys?" Crook pulled up a chair and signalled to the waiter to request two coffees.

"Dunno. There were a few of them with me when they threw us out. Where did you go?"

"I split when the windows got trashed at the Stardust and the riot squad showed up. Couldn't risk getting busted ahead of today."

Jimmy Dolan sat up and stretched then dry heaved into his hand.

"I can't face another day on the booze Crook. I'm dead, I'm going back to the flat for a kip."

"No, no, no, Brendan, I need you today. Go back, take a bath, have a shave, then straight back out. The guys said they'd meet at midday at the Sans Souci. We need to get there before then and have a full round of beers waiting for them when they arrive." Simeon Crook sat back as the waiter placed two coffee cups on the table. He then retrieved a sugar cube from a bowl and placed it on his saucer as Dolan sniffed at the coffee and recoiled.

"What's that?" Dolan squinted in the sunlight as Crook removed a small white crystal from a pill bottle with tweezers and placed it on the sugar cube.

"Medicine. Here swallow it down. You'll feel on top of the world in fifteen minutes."

Jimmy Dolan placed the sugar cube on his tongue and closed his eyes.

"Go on, swallow it."

Dolan grimaced and tipped back his head then retched.

"Good boy. You'll be fine now. Go back home and get cleaned up, then we go to the bar and get the guys some beers in before they arrive." Simeon Cook tilted the brown medicine bottle in the sunlight and smiled as he shook it.

"Those boys had a hard night, just like you. We need them to be raring to go today. They're going to need their medicine too!"

# Chapter 39

"Leeds...Leeds...Leeds." The slow rhythmic chant accompanied by a hammering of fists on the walls of the escalator echoed around Porte de Saint-Cloud metro station as thirty members of the LS9 Asylum ascended towards street level and clumsily vaulted the ticket barriers to emerge at a concrete traffic circle.

"There...touts!" Max Jackson pointed at two black youths in tracksuits standing in the centre of the dual carriageway and, with a roar, a dozen Englishmen charged towards them across the busy road.

The youths were immediately on their toes, sprinting away towards the Parc des Princes stadium.

"I told you there'd be loads of touts round here." Fat Lawrence grinned as Max and some of the younger lads gave chase.

"But guys, I have tickets, I told you..." Simeon Crook, gasping for breath at the back of the group, remained unheard as a group of Germans emerged from a sidestreet and were quickly scattered by another charge and a hail of bottles.

"Jimmy, wait....!" Crook raised an arm and signalled to Dolan to wait for him. "I'm thinking that second dose I dropped them might have been too much. They're going fucking crazy and there are still four hours to go until the game starts."

Jimmy Dolan doubled up laughing. "Come on Crook, what's the matter with you? You wanted a riot and these boys are already having one!"

"Yeah but we need it to happen inside the stadium. At this rate everyone will have been busted by the time the ballgame starts." Crook followed as the group barged through the double doors of a bistro with chequered table cloths and diners in suits and summer dresses, and Terry Jackson suddenly appeared behind the bar and started to fill a pint glass with Kronenbourg.

"I work in a pub, I'm going to give you a hand monsieur!" The young barman made a half-hearted attempt to push him away, then gave up as Eugene Wilson ducked through the gap in the counter and began to remove a brandy bottle from the optics. The barman shrugged and picked up the telephone as diners began to stand and abandon their still-full plates.

"Leeds United, Leeds United, We'll support you evermore!" Geoff clambered onto a table and pulled a yellow, blue and white balaclava over his face as Terry Jackson passed foam-filled half pint glasses across the bar to his friends.

"Ah fuck it, he's calling the cops." Simeon Crook peered into the restaurant from the doorway and shook his head.

"Might as well grab a beer before they get here then." Jimmy Dolan's eyes flashed red and he grinned and slapped Crook on the shoulder and pushed his way into the bar.

Alan Connolly closed his eyes as he felt the familiar surge of electricity coursing through his veins, until a wail of sirens cut through the noise of chanting and glass smashing. The American waved to him from the doorway and he took a swig from a brandy bottle and pushed through the crowd towards him.

"That's a CRS van, not normal police, it's the riot squad. Better get the guys ready to move." Crook glanced over his shoulder as the blue van took the roundabout on two screeching wheels and drove up the wrong side of the road towards them.

Alan Connolly took another mouthful of spirit and smiled. "You think one van is going to be able to shift this lot?"

The CRS officers were still pulling down the visors on their helmets as they exited through the rear doors of the van and were immediately back-pedalling under a hail of bottles and glasses. Non-Stop Nigel picked up a metal table from the pavement and staggered slowly forward with it suspended above his head, before heaving it towards the back doors of the van which were immediately pulled shut.

"Come on lads, they're backing off!" Alan Connolly swigged from the bottle before hurling it at the driver's side window of the van. A two-tone wail announced the arrival of another dark blue van which parked further down the road, and disgorged a squad of officers brandishing long truncheons and circular riot shields.

"Time to go lads!" Connolly shouted back into the bar and the LS9 Asylum spilled out clutching bottles of spirits and beer.

"I'm too fucking old for this." Simeon Crook ducked into a shop doorway and pulled on his shades, then quickly lit a cigarette and watched as the riot police pursued the scattering Leeds fans up the road.

Jimmy Dolan, running at the front of the retreating mob, paused and turned, took a swig from his beer bottle and launched it towards the advancing line of officers, then turned on his heels, catching the eye of Alan Connolly running alongside him.

"Jimmy next street, take a left!" Connolly darted between two parked cars and Dolan followed him off the main road and along a narrow avenue of shops selling baby clothes and sewing machines.

"Where did Crook go?" Dolan put his hands on his knees and bent double, gasping for breath.

"No idea, he was at the back. Didn't see him get nicked though."

Dolan straightened up and smiled after expelling a jet of snot from each nostril in turn.

"Don't worry about him. He'll talk his way out of it. He's seen far worse, believe me."

"Yeah he's certainly got a few tales to tell." Connolly breathed heavily and mopped at his brow as he watched police vans with flashing blue lights weaving through the traffic on the main road.

"He's taught me a lot, so he has." The two men began walking along the road, occasionally pausing to scan the dual carriageway behind them as another distant siren grew louder.

"There's a bar here, let's get a beer and let it calm down a bit. Can't risk you getting lifted." Connolly pointed to a bar-tabac on the corner of the street with a handful of streetside tables occupied by old men smoking roll-ups.

"Don't worry about me, I've been nicked loads of times."

"Yeah but if you get nicked here, they'll check your papers. Work out that you're not who you're meant to be. You can forget about going home then..." Alan Connolly pushed open the door and a bald-headed barman and two smokers leaning on the bar turned and glared at them.

"Yeah, well, about that..."

Alan Connolly held up two fingers and tapped on the Jupiler pump.

"About what?"

"About going home..." Dolan's eyes flicked between the barman and the two smokers who had fallen silent and were now staring at their ashtrays, and Alan Connolly felt his heart rate quicken.

"Don't worry about it. We'll breeze through customs, there's no way they'll be checking passports." Connolly blinked then smirked as the barman slammed a foaming half pint glass down too hard onto the bar in front of him.

"Yeah, I know...it's not that... You're not with them are you Alan?"

"Who? The Provos? No, not me. Got dragged into this whole thing by accident. Why?"

"Crook says they're going to kill me." Jimmy Dolan snatched at his beer before the barman had even placed it on the counter and swigged back half the glass.

"What? Why does he think that?" Connolly fought to suppress a wave of panic as he felt the electricity in his head fizz into life. *He's not as daft as he looks brother. The writing's on the wall and he knows it.*

"He says I'm in the same situation as he is with the CIA. We both know too much. Loose ends that need tying. Clearing the stable is what they call it."

Alan Connolly sipped at his beer and tried to stop his head from spinning. The barman muttered something to one of the smokers who looked sideways and laughed quietly.

"If they wanted you dead, why wouldn't they just get someone here to do it? Why go to the trouble of bringing you back?"

Jimmy Dolan shrugged. "I thought that too, but Crook reckons you never do a hit in a foreign country if you can do it at home. They have people on the inside in England and Ireland so can control it better. I don't know...what do you think Alan?"

Alan Connolly took a gulp of beer to drain his glass and narrowed his eyes as the two smokers now both laughed out loud at something the barman was saying. *He trusts you brother. You know the score, but are you going to tell him?*

"I don't know Jimmy, but you can't stay here forever, you'll have to go home sometime." Connolly reached into his leather jacket and felt the weight of the cold steel in the lining.

"But I wouldn't be here...Crook says I can join the RAD team. Travel the world with him, helping out on jobs. He's going to train me. That's what I want to do, so I'm sorry Alan, but I'm not going home on your bus tomorrow."

Alan Connolly breathed slowly in and out through his nose to try and control his breathing as the electricity surged, white light flashing bright behind his eyes. *It was always going to happen brother. Paris or fucking Belfast. No contest. Leaves you properly in the shite though.*

One of the smokers at the bar lifted his head to light a cigarette and this time he didn't look away. This time he raised his eyebrows and fixed Alan with a stare which asked what the fuck he was going to do about it.

"We'll talk about this later Jimmy. You go wait outside now."

Jimmy Dolan tipped back his glass and finished his beer, then headed to the door. Upon reaching the street, he glanced back through the glass to see Alan Connolly remove the bayonet from his jacket, then step over the smokers' upturned stools and slowly stride towards the fire escape through which the two men had fled. *Here we go brother, this is more like it. No surrender. No fucking surrender.*

# Chapter 40

"Come on, straight in, a couple of hundred of us. They won't know what's hit them." Max Jackson pulled the balaclava from his jacket and led Geoff and another dozen of the young lads through the crowds of Leeds fans towards the Carrefour supermarket on Boulevard Murat.

"Come on Leeds!" Geoff pulled on his balaclava and they jogged towards the double doors of the store where an old man in a blue overall was pushing a train of trolleys.

"Leeds! Leeds! Leeds!" The chant spread across the scrubby grass of the park and the group numbered around eighty when they burst through the doors and charged up the aisles, scattering tins and boxes as they headed towards the shelves stacked with alcohol.

"It's all going to kick off here. I don't want to get nicked before 'match, I'm off for a drink with 'old timers." Terry Jackson mopped at his brow and pointed down the road.

"Hang on Terry, I'll join you." Alan Connolly picked up a bottle from a crate of Kronenbourg on the grass and twisted off the top. "Where are they?"

"Little bar round 'corner. Gene and Fat Lawrence and that Yank are in there. He's full of it him int' he?"

"What do you mean?" Connolly glanced back over his shoulder as the wail of sirens announced the arrival of three CRS vans.

"Some of 'tales he tells. I thought Eugene could talk but he's got nowt on this lad."

Simeon Crook removed his shades and raised them in a salute as Connolly and Jackson rounded the corner.

"Alan, grab a beer my friend, pull up a chair."

Eugene Wilson and Fat Lawrence turned awkwardly and squinted into the sun and swayed in their seats as they greeted the new arrivals.

"Alan..Alan..listen to this. Simon here, you won't believe this what he's been telling us..."

"Simeon. Simeon Crook III." Crook lifted his hand and waggled his fingers to attract Wilson's attention.

"Yeah, yeah, whatever you want pal...listen to this Alan. Man on 'moon, 1969, remember? Well..." Eugene Wilson gestured towards Crook with an open palm.

Simeon Crook replaced his shades and swilled and sniffed at a brandy bowl in his hand.

"Go on. Tell him Simon."

"Later. It's not important."

"You didn't go to 'moon too did you kid?" Terry Jackson slapped Crook on the back as he sat down and Fat Lawrence and Wilson cackled with laughter.

"No. No one did. We faked it." Crook muttered under his breath as Alan Connolly leant in towards him.

"I need a word inside."

Crook picked up a packet of Gauloises and the brandy glass and followed Connolly towards two high stools at the bar.

"How's things buddy? Any more of the boys been busted yet?"

"I've lost count to be honest. I think the beer must be stronger here than at home."

"Yeah, sure is. Well known for it. Sends us Americans crazy, that's why I stick to this." Crook raised his glass.

"I've got a problem..." Alan Connolly reached slowly across and removed Crook's mirror shades then handed them back to him, and looked hard into his eyes. "I was talking to Jimmy earlier. He thinks the IRA are going to kill him when he gets back to England."

"Highly likely in my opinion. Surely that's his problem though, not yours." Crook took the sunglasses and placed them in the top pocket of his shirt.

"I've been given a job, to get him back into England. If he doesn't come back, I've failed and believe me, that's a problem." Connolly tried to maintain eye contact but Crook's eyes flitted from the bar to the door then down to his tan Cuban heel boots.

"So what do you want me to do? Want me to lie to the kid, tell him it will all be okay, when I know it won't? Is that what you fucking want me to do Alan?" Crook pushed back the barstool and now met Connolly's glare with one of his own.

"You don't know for sure what will happen, maybe they just want..."

"I don't know? I don't fucking know Alan? Really? This is my life, my reality. I live it every day. Loose ends. Cleaning the stable. And you think I don't know?" Crook's raised voice caused three heads to turn from the pavement table.

"Okay, I get it. I'm sorry. I just wish you hadn't said it. Let Jimmy make up his own mind."

"I'm looking out for the kid Alan. He's a rookie, I'm not. I say it how I see it."

Alan Connolly tried to speak but his mouth was too dry and his legs wobbled when he tried to get off the stool. His head pounded but this time it felt different to the usual hum of electricity, and he tried to remember how much he'd had to drink. *Not pished are you brother? Fucking lightweight.*

"Anyway...Mick Jagger." Simeon Crook smiled and positioned himself back on the barstool. "Garcon, two more."

"What about him?"

"I never finished my story."

"I don't think it matters now." Alan Connolly leant on the bar and fought the urge to vomit.

"Aw come on...I'll tell you the story anyway. I think you'll enjoy this one, it's a real doozie."

# Chapter 41

Simeon Crook swigged back the remaining brandy in his glass and grimaced then picked up a full one from the bar.

"Okay, so back in 69, Reagan, you know, the cowboy actor guy, him and Nixon got involved in a playground squabble. Reagan was running for re-election as California governor on a low tax, low crime ticket. Nixon was trying to push through some welfare reforms, and the cowboy was hollering in the press, accusing Dicky of going soft, turning into some fucking pinko socialist. Nixon got real pissed and decided we needed to derail the Cowboy's governorship campaign. Fuck up his low-crime Cali vision was the plan. You following so far?" Simeon Crook was on his feet, pacing the bar, hands gesticulating wildly, then scratching at his moustache.

"I was inside in '69." Alan Connolly swayed on his barstool then picked up a glass of brandy from the bar and sniffed at it suspiciously.

"Irrelevant...so there was me and another guy from the company running the op. The bosses said just go do your own thing, we were totally off the leash, man. So my buddy Joey was from the South, Alabama, and he got this idea to light a big fire under Reagan's ass, the biggest. One that would burn right through to the election in '70. A fucking race war! Blacks v whites! He would get the whites all riled up, I'd do the same with the blacks. So, Joey pulled in his boy Charlie and told him the plan. Kill whitey and point the finger at the negro. Fucking Helter Skelter coming down fast and all the rest of that shit, you know the story..."

"Wait a minute, are you talking about Manson?" Alan Connolly sat up straighter on his barstool and closed his eyes to stop the room spinning.

"Charlie, yeah. Fucking loose cannon that cat, always took things too far, I never trusted the little fucker." Simeon Crook rested his brandy glass on the bar long enough to light a cigarette and position it in the corner of his mouth.

"Manson was working for the government?"

"No, not the government, the company. Same but different, okay?"

"Not really but carry on." Connolly sipped at his brandy and gagged.

"Anyway, forget Manson, that was Joey. My plan was even better. I was going to try to get both the blacks and the whites all riled up. So your guy Jagger, he had a problem. The Stones were slated to play 24 concerts across the states in late' 69 but he had a drug conviction after the party with the chick and the fur rug and the candy bar, you remember?"

"The Redlands raid in 67, yeah of course."

"So Jagger and Richards couldn't get a visa. Big problem, no visa, no tour, no mega bucks merchandising score. So I offered them a deal. That's how they got in."

"So what was the deal?" Connolly was now holding the brandy glass in both hands, swaying on his barstool as he leaned in towards Crook.

"Here's where I got real creative! I had a loose end of my own I needed tying up. Some shit to clear from my own stable if you will. This black kid Hunter from Berkeley, he'd done a few jobs for me but he'd started to run his mouth when he was high, which was most of the time. I needed rid of him. I told him that the politicians thought that Jagger was a corrupting influence on the youth of our great nation, and it had been decided he needed taking out. I would set up a situation where Hunter could do the job and get clean away after, no problem. An open air concert, a sort of west coast Woodstock, but it would be badly organised and totally chaotic.

"Altamont?"

"Exactly. The Altamont Speedway free concert. It was perfect. Next to the Freeway so all the freaks could easily get there from Frisco and Oakland, there would be gridlock on surrounding roads and the local hick towns would be overwhelmed by stoned fucking hippies. I'd use a low stage, easy access for a shooter, and the best bit of all...I'd get the fucking Hells Angels to run security and pay them from my stash of confiscated pot and acid. I spent weeks setting that shit up. You couldn't fucking make up something so perfect man!"

"Wait, so Jagger would get his visa but he was going to have to get assassinated for it?"

"No buddy, no. I haven't got to that yet. This is the clever part. The gun I gave Hunter wouldn't fire. He'd make the assassination attempt in full view of the press cameras, the whole world would see some crazy Black Panther supporter try to kill His Satanic Majesty, whitey's new king of pop music. Even the fucking hippies would turn on the blacks after that. Plus, the Angels had the green light to take that motherfucker down hard."

"Which they did. Stabbed and stomped him to death." Connolly puffed out his cheeks and shook his head.

"A loose end tied up for me, plus it would get the blacks all riled up too. Hunter dead. Hippies hating on the blacks, the negro hating fucking whitey more than ever. It was absolute fucking perfection man!"

"And Jagger went along with all that?"

"He had to. The tour manager Cutler made him. There was too much cash at stake for him not to get that visa. Problem was Jagger lost his nerve the night before. I ended up holding him in that motel bathroom as he cried like a baby, shaking with fear."

"Where was this?" Alan Connolly rubbed at his temples, a low hum in his brain making it hard to concentrate.

"In Tracy, near Altamont. He was scared the gun would go off. I held him and stroked that beautiful hair and I saw then that the tough guy front is all just a big act. Told him it would all be okay. That when he started singing 'Satisfaction' that would be the sign for Hunter to try to take the shot, but it wouldn't happen. That the Angels would take care of the shooter."

"So what happened?" Connolly sat back on the barstool and dipped his top lip into the brandy. "It all went down as you planned didn't it? So why didn't the race war start?"

"Well Charlie and the girls screwed up Joey's operation by going off plan to settle some stupid fucked-up grudge. My plan just worked too well. Three hundred thousand people turned up at Altamont. Three hundred thousand! I was expecting fifty at most. Then the Angels went fucking berserk, rode their bikes to the front of the stage and beat on everyone in sight with billy clubs. There was a ton of bad acid around, kids tripping out all over the field. One kid thought he was a fucking dophin and drowned in the moat. Two more killed by a farm truck while they were asleep in the road. The Grateful Dead were so freaked out by what was happening they jumped on a chopper and got the hell out of there. Hunter Meredith was so stoned he didn't even point the gun at Jagger, just waved it around in front of the stage so no one even knew what he was trying to do. Some crazy black motherfucker getting lynched by Sonny Barger and his boys in amongst all that chaos was never going to make more than page 2 news. Who even gave a fuck in the end?"

Simeon Crook strode back and forth along the length of the bar, his raised voice causing the three heads to turn again from the pavement table.

"Dick Helms hauled Joey and me in, busted both are asses. A perfect plan, worked too well and we ended up being the bad guys again. It was all so fucking unfair man!"

Alan Connolly stepped from the barstool and reached across with a trembling hand to take the mirror shades from Crook's shirt pocket. He carefully unfolded them and slowly replaced them on the bridge of the American's nose, then stared at his own red eyed reflection and smiled.

"I bet Meredith Hunter thought it was all pretty unfair too...just before they killed him."

## Chapter 42

*It's Bayern Munich kicking off the 20th European cup final in Paris... Tremendous support for Leeds behind the goal they're defending... There certainly seem to be more than 8000 Leeds fans here... Andersson is stretchered off after just 3 minutes following that tackle by Yorath...Great shot, just over the bar from Hunter... Lorimer, just wide... Leeds have definitely got this game in complete control in the opening minutes..*

"Guys – take a beer. It's crazy down under the stand. Your hooligans have taken over the bar. The bar tenders have given up on collecting any money. Free drinks all round! Play up Leeds, shoot for the endzone boys!"

*Lorimer, thirty yards out, picks up a loose ball. Lorimer drops his shoulder, dribbles past one defender, past two defenders, into the penalty area. Beckenbauer goes to ground. Ball bounces off Beckenbauer's left hand... Lorimer appeals... Referee waves play on.*

"Fucking penalty. It hit his hand! The ref was right there, how could he not see that? Cheating French bastard!"

*Ball knocked forward by Giles. Controlled nicely by Clarke. Beckenbauer standing him up. Clarke drives left into the area. Clarke bearing down on the six yard box. Clarke still going. Clarke pulls back his left leg to shoot. Brilliant play by Clarke... and is that a penalty?? No! The referee has pointed to the corner. Beckenbauer didn't like that situation, it looked a definite penalty to me, Clarke was clean through and Beckenbauer clearly took his right leg out from under him.*

"Fucking hell! Fucking hell! Penalty! He got nowhere near 'ball. How can he not give that? He said it, that yank. He said last night that 'Corsican mafia have put money on 'krauts to win. They've got to that bastard ref, I tell you!"

*Second half... Giles with the free kick. Floated into Madeley, who hasn't been picked up at the back. Header into the box.. cleared... only to... Lorimer! First time volley straight into the roof of the net! 1-0 Leeds!*

"Yeeessssss! Get in! Have that you cheating Nazi bastards! Go on Leeds! Yessssss! Leeds Leeds Leeds!"

*And the German players are protesting. Beckenbauer is complaining to the linesman. And what's the referee given? See what happened here. Madeley knocked it back into the box.. Lorimer put it away... And Bremner may have been offside... And while you're watching the replay there's bedlam on the pitch... Photographers on the pitch, the Leeds players pointing to the linesman who has gone back to the halfway line... Zobel shoving Yorath. Maier jostling with Bremner. The linesman has no doubt... What's the referee given? The referee who seems to have had his problems, has now given a goal.... Total confusion and...No, no he hasn't, he's given offside. The goal won't stand. Bremner offside is the decision. No goal.*

"What?? What?! He's fucking disallowed it. I don't believe it. It's fucking robbery, that's what it is. You cheating bastard! Come on Leeds, on the fucking pitch!"

*71 minutes... Floated pass over the top by Muller...nicely weighted pass from Torstenson. Franz Roth running at Madeley... Madeley back pedalling. Drilled shot from Roth..through Madeley's legs and past Stewart into the left hand corner of the Leeds net. It's 1-0 Bayern.*

"Stamp on 'seats, they break off easy. Go on lads, get over 'fence. Gelderd Aggro! Gelderd Aggro! There's gonna be a riot!"

*Bit of trouble behind the goal where most of the Leeds supporters are, and objects are being thrown onto the grass behind the goal... It really is sad, I presume the Leeds fans feel badly done to after Lorimer put the ball in the net but it was disallowed... Police in riot gear now gathering in front of the Leeds fans.*

"The CRS are here! Give it to them with 'seats lads. We'll get those fuckers back for earlier. Gelderd Aggro! Asylum Aggro!"

*81 minutes...A Leeds fan now being removed from the pitch by stewards in tracksuits... Jupp Kapplemen with a good run on the right..closely watched by Frank Gray and Hunter.. Kapplemen with the cross... Muller pulls away from Madeley in the 6 yard box. 2-0! Surely that is the end for Leeds... Terrible scenes behind the goal on the right now, debris showering down onto the pitch.*

"Leeds United, Leeds United, we'll support you ever more... Fuck off you cheating German bastards!"

*It looks like one of those nights when nothing will go for Leeds... Again here they are in a major final, again seeing the game ebbing away from them even though they've had so much of the play... Bayern Munich have retained the European Cup... It's a really sad evening for Leeds."*

"This is carnage Brendan, pure carnage! These Leeds boys haven't let us down. This is going to be front page news right round the world. No chance of them moving the world series to France now! Job done buddy, and the night isn't over yet!"

# Chapter 43

"So that was their team bus then Crook?" Max Jackson dabbed at a crimson wound on his scalp with a blood-stained Leeds scarf.

"Sure it was buddy. Not a fucking pane of glass left in that son-of-a-bitch when you guys were done with it!" Simeon Crook grinned and slapped Max on the back, then squeezed the skinny arse of a passing girl in a spangled leotard.

"How did you know where the Germans' bus was parked?" Jimmy Dolan swayed, eyes half-closed, on a barstool at the Taxi Girls club.

Simeon Crook cupped his hand to Dolan's ear.

"It wasn't the Munich bus Brendan. It was the bus the soccer suits used to get from the hotel. The football federation high-ups, whatever they call themselves. All they'll remember is a cold ride home on a busted up bus when they discuss whether to shift that 78 World Series to France in a few months."

Crook raised his glass and nudged Dolan to half-heartedly lift his own.

"Looks like the old medicine is starting to wear off." Crook smiled as he observed a dozen sleeping members of the LS9 Asylum slumped on the low sofas surrounding the club's small dancefloor.

"Mine is too. I feel fucked." Dolan's chin drooped towards his chest and his full glass wobbled precariously in his shaking hand.

"It's a job well done tonight Brendan. You go back to the room, get some sleep. We need to be up and away before Connolly comes looking for you tomorrow."

Jimmy Dolan shuffled slowly from his seat.

"I'll just say goodnight to the boys."

"No Brendan, just go. If Connolly asks I'll say I don't know where you are. I'll keep them drinking here for a few hours. See you back at the room."

Jimmy Dolan nodded and stood swaying in front of Crook, then extended his hand.

"Thanks Crook."

Simeon Crook took his hand and gripped it hard.

"No problem buddy. Here's to a good night's work and to new beginnings. Here's to the newest member of RAD team!"

# Chapter 44

Simeon Crook didn't need to turn round to know that Alan Connolly was approaching from behind. Norman and Scotty shifted their focus from his eyes to somewhere over his shoulder and their expressions told him that it didn't appear to be good news.

"Alan...drink?" Connolly remained silent, his eyes flashing in time with the lights in the club. Red. Orange. Green.

"A word." Connolly nodded towards the bar and Norman and Scotty took a step back.

"I know the owner here. Good job too. Most of the city is locked down..." Crook signalled to the barman with two fingers then leant on the bar, turning to face the room.

"So who are you then?" Connolly was in front of him, a silhouette in the flashing lights, his face concealed in shadow.

"Excuse me?"

"Who are you, really?" The barman appeared over Crook's shoulder, an ice cube suspended over the brandy glass. Alan Connolly nodded and waved him away.

Simeon Crook was avoiding eye contact, his face alternately bright and dark. Red. Orange. Green.

"What do you mean Alan, you know who I am..."

"Aye, Simeon Crook the third." Alan took a step closer, the ambiguous smile returning to his face.

"Sure, you know that." Crook turned to pick up a glass of brandy from the bar.

Connolly pulled a barstool alongside Crook, then leant in towards him, raising his voice to be heard above the exploding chorus of 'Jet' by Wings.

"You fucked up old son."

"Huh? Sorry buddy, I don't know what you mean." Crook swilled the brandy in its bowl and sniffed at it without turning to face Connolly.

"CIA...killing presidents...fake moon landings...I don't know anything about any of that. Maybe it's real, maybe it's a pile of shite, I really don't know..."

Crook took a swig of his drink and scratched at his moustache and leant in to reply but Alan Connolly raised his index finger to stop him.

"I'd have believed all that stuff, just like Jimmy did, but where you fucked up, where you really blew the whole thing, was involving the Stones."

"The Stones?" Crook laughed like he didn't mean it and chewed on a fingernail buried deep in his moustache.

"Yep, the Stones. You know why that blew it Simon, or whatever it is you're calling yourself?"

"That whole Stones thing, it was years ago man..." Crook tipped back his glass and drained it in a single gulp.

"You fucked up because you told that story to someone who knows everything about the Stones. Every small detail of their history. Being locked up for twenty three hours a day does that to you, you become obsessive. You read every newspaper article, remember every story you hear on the radio. Some of the boys inside collect wank mags, some spend all day gambling, some build a fucking model of York Minster out of matches. Me, I just read everything I could about the Rolling Stones."

Simeon Crook fell silent and closed his eyes, rocking slowly back and forth on the barstool.

"You want to know which bits you fucked up on then?"

Simeon Crook opened his eyes and breathed heavily and loudly and shook his head, but Alan Connolly was off his stool, grinning as he paced the length of the bar.

"Fuck up number one!" Connolly raised his index finger and held it in front of Crook's nose. "You said it took you weeks to set up Altamont. Wrong! Up until two days before the concert, it was due to be held at Sonoma. The owner there asked for a one hundred grand upfront surety and it was switched at the last minute."

Crook licked at his lips and picked up his empty glass, willing it to be full again.

"Fuck up number two! You said Jagger was crying in a motel in Tracy the night before the concert. Wrong! The Stones stayed at the Huntington in San Francisco that night. Everyone knows that. It's pretty much common knowledge, so you haven't even done your research properly. Pretty lazy that, Simon."

Crook looked over his shoulder, searching in vain for the barman who was collecting empty glasses from tables supporting the heads of sleeping Leeds fans.

"Hey, I haven't finished yet! Fuck up number three...You said the signal for Meredith Hunter to try to take the shot at Jagger was when the band played 'Satisfaction'. Wrong! They were playing 'Sympathy for the Devil' when he started waving the gun around."

Alan Connolly paused and smiled , then took a step forward and placed a firm hand on the American's shoulder.

"So, Simon, we seem to have exposed a number of flaws in that particular story, which if I'm honest, was probably one of the more believable ones you've been telling everyone here. So, I'll ask you again. Who are you? And before you answer, please believe me when I tell you that people generally only lie to me once. Once, I can accept as a mistake. Twice, is a sign of great disrespect where I come from, and I don't tolerate being disrespected. Understand?"

Connolly moved his hand to below the American's chin and slowly lifted it from his chest until their eyes met, two feet apart, light then dark in the flashing lights. Red, Orange, Green.

"Go on then. Time for the truth. Who are you really?"

The American closed his eyes then raised his hands to his face and rocked back and forth on the barstool.

"Fuck's sake son, don't cry. I can't do with that shite." Alan Connolly pulled himself back onto his stool and picked up his brandy from the bar, took a swig then passed it to the American who downed it in one gulp.

"Jesus...I'm sorry. It just...just all got out of hand."

Connolly nodded to the barman and held up two fingers.

"I didn't mean to cause any trouble..."

"Trouble? Fuck's sake son, if young Jimmy doesn't get on my bus tomorrow, it'll be more than trouble. I'm fucking dead, or nicked, or maybe somehow even both. So yeah,

I'd say your bullshit has certainly caused some trouble. So help me out. Who are you and why did you do it?"

The American shook his head and sobbed gently as he turned to take a brandy glass from the barman.

"I guess I was lonely. Got laid off two years ago, been looking after my mom since then. She died back in the Fall. I sold the house, split the cash with my sister, and I just decided to take off, travel a little, see Europe. I've always dreamt of coming to France. I even did a night school class to learn a bit of the language."

"No wife or kids?" Alan Connolly ran his finger around the rim of his glass without turning to face the American.

"Split with my wife twenty years back. There's been no one since. My name's Gary by the way, Gary Blickenstorfer."

The American extended his hand towards Connolly, who paused before shaking it.

"I sold insurance products. Same company for 23 years, until I got bombed out. When my mom died, I just thought, what am I doing here? I'm fifty next year. It's time to make something of my life. I'd always wanted to see Europe, but when I got here, it was different, sure, but deep down it was really just the same as being at home. I was still on my own, still nobody gave a shit about me."

"Until you became Simeon Crook, the retired spy."

Gary Blickenstorfer nodded his head and rubbed at his eyes.

"I'd seen Jimmy drinking alone in the Sans Souci. We'd said a few hellos but I didn't know how to start a conversation. Five minutes of hearing about my boring life and he'd just take off. I love reading – spy stuff, espionage, conspiracies. Forsyth, Fleming, Ludlum, all that stuff. So I invented Crook, and you know what, I fucking loved being that guy! I lived more in the few weeks I've been Simeon Crook than I have in my whole life. It was like he took over and somehow made everything better!"

Connolly stared ahead as Max Jackson lifted his head from one of the tables and vomited spectacularly across the small dancefloor.

"Aye, he was a fun guy alright. But unfortunately Gary, Simeon Crook has to die now."

"What do you mean?" Blickenstorfer turned slowly to face him.

"Well, our mutual friend Simeon Crook has put the idea into Jimmy's head that he's going to be killed if he gets on that bus with me. So we need to change that idea before tomorrow. Correction, you need to change that idea, or I'm in big trouble. Which means you are too. So basically, it's Crook or you son."

Gary Blickenstorfer nodded slowly.

"So Crook has to die?"

Alan Connolly took a swig of his drink.

"I'm afraid so Gary. And I'll tell you how we're going to kill him."

# Chapter 45

"Wake up Jimmy." The dark figure was sat on a dining chair facing his bed when Jimmy Dolan woke up in the attic bedsit on Rue Jean-Baptiste.

"Who's that?" Dolan pulled himself upright and tugged on a cord above his head and the room's bare bulb flicked into life.

"Alan...what are you doing here? Where's Crook?"

Alan Connolly stood and approached the bed, an envelope in his hand.

"I have some bad news Jimmy."

"What...? What happened? Has Crook been arrested?"

"No, it's worse than that." Connolly placed the envelope on the bed and sat back down on the chair.

"Oh fuck no, the company, they caught up with him, shit, no, don't say that Alan..."

"It's not that either Jimmy. Just read the letter." Connolly folded his arms and his eyes scanned the room, his nose twitching and top lip curling involuntarily.

Jimmy Dolan swang his legs from the bed and sat in his red underpants, turning the envelope in his hand.

"What's it say?"

"It's addressed to you son. How the fuck do I know what it says. He asked me to bring it to you."

"But where is he? He's meant to be here..."

"Just read the fucking letter Jimmy! Jesus..." Connolly stood and walked over to the sink, then opened the fridge and closed it again quickly. "Do you know there's maggots in there?"

Jimmy Dolan shook his head and tore open the envelope and began to read aloud to himself.

"*Dear Brendan*...He always calls me Brendan you know?"

"Yeah. Fucking weird if you ask me." Alan Connolly leant on the sink and checked his watch.

"*Dear Brendan. I've done a very bad thing. A terrible thing in fact. I lied to you buddy. My name isn't Simeon Crook III, and I wasn't*...fuck." Jimmy Dolan turned the letter over and placed it on the bed as his face crumpled and tears began to streak his cheeks.

"Yeah, he told me. His name was Gary. He was an insurance salesman."

Jimmy Dolan sank backwards onto the bed, his hands covering his face and loud sobs filled the room.

"Why? Why did he lie to me?"

"Same reason anyone lies. To impress you, keep you interested." Alan Connolly walked to the bed and picked up the letter and began to read it aloud.

"*I wasn't in the CIA. I didn't kill the Australian Prime Minister or threaten the referee in the soccer game. Every single thing I told you was a lie. I'm just a normal guy, not a spy. I can't put into words how sorry I am and I hope you can find it in your heart to forgive me.*"

"No stop...fucking hell Alan, I don't want to hear anymore." Jimmy Dolan turned and buried his face in the pillow and Alan Connolly looked down at his trembling body as he wept in loud gasps.

"There's a bit more. It's important so I'll read this...*There is no CIA contract on me. No RAD team. No loose ends and no cleaning the stable. Don't let my awful lies stop you from going home. You aren't in any danger, so go back to your family Brendan and enjoy the rest of your life. With fond memories, from your friend, Simeon Crook III*....and there's a PS. It says... *there's a brown envelope under the doormat with some cash and the photos I've taken during our vacation. I'd like you to have them and maybe remember the good times we shared together.*"

"Fuck off Crook. You're a fucking liar and I hate you." Jimmy Dolan sobbed into his pillow and Alan Connolly placed the letter beside him.

"I'll kip here tonight if that's okay Jimmy? Then in the morning we'll collect the boys who got nicked and get out of Paris. I doubt we're going to be very popular round here after last night. We'll be back in England this time tomorrow and you'll be on your way home."

# Chapter 46

## Thursday 29 March 1975, Calais

*Shame of Paris – Many Leeds fans arrived back in England today disgusted at the behaviour of some British supporters at last night's European cup final in Paris. Several said they doubted if the troublemakers were genuine Leeds fans. United were beaten 2-0 by Bayern Munich. Eleven Britons were taken to hospital, as was a French cameraman who suffered a serious eye injury. There was no information on the condition of a French ticket tout who was left bleeding on a street corner near the stadium after Leeds fans had robbed and beaten him.*

"Great idea to stay in Paris last night Al. There's lads on this boat who got to Calais last night. 500 of them have being kipping in railway carriages because of 'strike." Norman spat from the top deck of the ferry as it slowly negotiated its way out of the French port.

"They've just opened 'Duty Free an' all." Scotty reeled across the deck clutching a Sealink carrier bag and swigging from a can of Heineken.

"Here's the kid. He'll tell you." Dennis Copley led two youths in LUFC patch-covered denim jackets towards Jimmy Dolan sitting on the deck, his back to the railing and his head in his hands.

"Jimmy, tell these two what your mate told us..."

"What?" Dolan looked up and squinted into the weak sun through red eyes.

"Costa Rican mafia wasn't it? Who bribed 'ref."

"Corsican mafia you fucking idiot." Norman turned, laughing.

"Aye, well it were 'mafia anyway. Bribed 'ref. Some betting scam his mate said. He were bent, 100%. Tell 'em what he said kid." Copley tapped at Jimmy Dolan's black baseball boot with his own block-toed two-tone brogue.

The two youths in the denim jackets looked down at Dolan, who shook his head and buried his face in his hands.

"His mate were into some proper dodgy stuff. Knew everyone in Paris. He'd heard before 'game that mafia had got to 'ref..." As Copley spoke, Jimmy Dolan suddenly hauled himself to his feet, breathing heavily, with tears streaking his cheeks in the faint sunlight and thrust his face towards Copley's.

"Fucking stop talking about it! He was a fucking liar alright? The ref wasn't bent. It was a lie, just like everything else."

Copley took a step back and shrugged at the two youths as Jimmy Dolan strode away down the deck.

"Don't know what's up with him. Anyway, I know what I saw, that ref were bent, end of."

"He's upset. Had a bad night." Alan Connolly winked at Copley and followed Dolan along the deck.

Reaching the railing at the stern of the ferry, Jimmy Dolan could go no further and stood with his chin resting on his arms, watching the beaches of Northern France shrink away into the distance.

"You alright Jimmy? You were quiet on the bus." Alan Connolly joined him on the railing and gazed down into the churning wake sixty feet below.

"What do you think?"

"I think you're going home mate, see your mam and dad again. No checks at Calais and they'll just want this lot through as quick as possible at Dover. No problem."

Jimmy Dolan remained silent and shook his head.

"The pick-up place is only twenty minutes from the ferry. You'll be at the safe house in time for your dinner." Connolly patted him on the back.

"Yeah, maybe."

"Come on son, what Crook said was bollocks. He was a fucking insurance man, what did he know? You'll be fine. Trust me."

Jimmy Dolan turned to face Connolly, his lip trembling and Connolly avoided his stare.

"Want a coffee? I'm going for one." Connolly reached into his leather jacket to retrieve his wallet.

"Oh, and there's this."

He handed a thick brown envelope to Dolan.

"It's what Crook left under the mat. Even if you don't want the photos, he said there was some cash in it didn't he?"

Dolan took the envelope in his hand and stared at it.

"See you back here in a minute. Black coffee, loads of sugar, that will sort you out son."

# Chapter 47

Alan Connolly cursed as scalding coffee splashed onto his fingers as he tried to match his steps along the gangway with the pitches and rolls of the ferry. *Nearly there now brother. Stick the kid at the back of the bus at customs and you're home and dry. Job done.*

Through the metal door, with the chilly Channel wind whipping the froth off the top of the coffee cups and onto the backs of his hands. Stomach churning as he glanced right to see the navy blue ocean far below. Staggering like a drunk in response to the movement of the ship, left to right to left as he made his way to the back of the boat. Eyes moving from the coffee cups in his hands to his feet on the deck, then reaching the stern, looking up to see Jimmy Dolan sat on the top of the railing, legs swinging, facing down, staring at the deck. *Here we go brother. Something not quite right here.*

"Jimmy...careful mate. What are you doing up there?"

Jimmy Dolan looked up, his hands on the railing. He shook his head and smiled a smile that wasn't one.

Twenty feet away, Alan Connolly stopped, the steaming coffee cups in his hands.

"Get down mate, you're making me nervous sitting up there."

Jimmy Dolan reached into his denim jacket and removed the brown envelope and began to laugh.

Jimmy Dolan held the brown envelope in front of him, then tossed it down onto the deck.

Jimmy Dolan shook his head, no longer smiling, no longer laughing. Alan Connolly stooped to slowly place the coffee cups on the deck, then stood, his arms outstretched, palms facing down.

"Jimmy...Jimmy...come on son..."

Jimmy Dolan tilted his head and looked up at the sky. Jimmy Dolan took his hands from the railings. Jimmy Dolan leant backwards, watching his own feet rising above his head as he tumbled backwards off the rail.

"No! No! Fucking no!" Alan Connolly dashed forward, his feet sending the contents of the paper cups splashing across the deck and up his legs, hot coffee scalding his shins. Hands on the railing, his eyes scanned the white foam of the wake in the navy blue sea.

"Jimmy! Jimmy! Fucking hell, no!"

Jimmy Dolan's head appeared as a small black dot in the white wake for a second, two seconds, three seconds, then Jimmy Dolan was gone.

Alan Connolly gripped the railing which stopped his hands shaking, but only made the rest of his body convulse even more. The electricity fizzed and crackled in his brain, the white noise flashing and sparking. When he puked through his mouth and his nose, the wind blew it back into his eyes and blinded him.

*This is it brother. This. Is. It. Fucked. Absolutely fucked.*

Alan Connolly wiped the vomit from his face and slumped onto the deck below a lifebelt cabinet, finally managing to catch his breath now he was away from the wind. His heart pounded so hard in his chest that it hurt and his hand shook so much he could barely take hold of the brown envelope which lay on the deck beside him.

His trembling fingers took a few seconds to negotiate the ripped opening of the envelope and remove a clip of brand new Franc notes, secured by a paper clip. Alan Connolly thrust the notes into the pocket of his jacket and tipped the remaining contents of the envelope onto the deck.

Connolly ignored the silver chain with a St. Christopher pendant, and picked up a bundle of colour photographs. Removing the rubber band which held them together, Connolly's shaking hand flicked through the collection. Paris in the spring...the Eiffel Tower, boats on the Seine, churches, a solitary drink on a table at a pavement café, the stories of a holiday spent alone.

Then the tousled hair, smiling eyes and scruffy denim of Jimmy Dolan. Jimmy eating an ice cream, Jimmy in front of a cathedral, Jimmy with a beer, Jimmy rowing a boat, Jimmy with a brandy. The stories of a holiday with a friend.

Then a photo of a building, single storey, made of brick. A photo out of place in this collection. No architectural or historical merit, no recollection of good times well spent. Just a brick built, flat roofed building in a French suburb, surrounded by low trees. Alan Connolly held it closer in his trembling fingers to read a blue sign in the right hand corner. 'Ecole Primaire La Milliere de Marseille'. A photo of Jimmy Dolan grinning, pointing at the sign for Pigalle Metro. Jimmy with another beer. An elderly woman pulling a shopping trolley beneath a sign saying SUPER-U. The same old woman loading groceries into the boot of a red Citroen 2CV. Alan Connolly studied the photo, then turned it over to read the biro scrawl on the back. 'Madame Salomon. Super-U supermarket. Rue St.Pierre, Marseille. 5/13/75.' Jimmy Dolan alongside a gargoyle on the roof of a cathedral overlooking the Seine. A woman in her late thirties in flared corduroys and a yellow cardigan, standing outside the single storey, brick-built building with two other women. The same three women from a different angle, closer this time.

Alan Connolly turned the photo in fingers which now shook and pulsed with electricity.

'His wife. School pick up. 5/14/75.'

The woman in the flared cords and the yellow cardigan stooping to speak to a blonde 6-year-old in a red summer dress. The woman in the cords and the blonde girl standing with a group of women and children outside the single storey brick building. The woman and the blonde girl and a curly haired boy, a couple of years younger than the girl, walking in front of the single storey, brick built building.

Alan Connolly felt the electricity surging through his body, the phosphorescent glow of white light burning in his brain. His trembling fingers slowly turned the photo to read the biro writing on the reverse.

'Referee Saloman's wife and children. La Milliere primary school Marseille. 5/14/75.'

Alan Connolly tossed the pile of photos onto the deck and watched as they were picked up by the wind and blown through the railing, disappearing into the foaming wake which had consumed Jimmy Dolan. Connolly sat on the deck and looked upwards and screamed at the sky to drown out the hum of the electricity and the voice of his brother, too loud to ignore.. *Don't look brother. What good will it do now? It's over. You know it is.*

Alan Connolly slowly reached down and picked up the St. Christopher pendant between his thumb and index finger. He held it up to the light, and stared at the embossed silver figure brandishing a staff , carrying a small child upon his shoulder. *Just put it down. No good can come of it brother. No point looking. It's over.*

Alan Connolly felt the weight of the pendant in his palm and the surge of electricity slowly subsided, and the fizz and crackle became a low hum as he clenched his fist, holding it tight. He paused, waiting for his brother's voice but all he could hear was the drone of the ship's engine and the crashing of the waves and the wind whistling across the deck. He opened his palm then turned the pendant in his shaking fingers to read the words inscribed on the back of the disc.

"To Simeon. Happy 13th birthday. 12 Oct 1939. Love Mom and Brendan."

# Chapter 48

**Wednesday 28 April 1982, Leeds**

*Crunch Game for United – Relegation haunted Leeds United face a tough challenge at Villa Park tonight with a visit to European Cup finalists Aston Villa. Second from bottom United are in desperate need of points but know that their relegation fate is still in their own hands with three games in hand on fourth bottom Wolves who are only two points ahead of the Whites.*

He was sat on the bench, where he always sat. Round the corner, behind the rubbish bins, in a small brick courtyard which offered some protection from the chill Spring winds which blew down the Aire Valley and penetrated the grey Victorian citadel of Armley Jail. He knew that on the rare occasions there was a break in the grey cloud cover, a narrow shaft of sunlight would illuminate this bleak square for a fleeting moment. So now he sat, eyes closed and face tilted upwards, enjoying the unfamiliar sensation of warm, natural light on his face, not noticing as the other man approached across the empty exercise yard.

Alan Connolly clutched the pencil in his right hand, concealed in the pocket of his overalls, slowly increasing the pressure on the sharp lead tip with his thumb until he felt the sticky warmth of blood spreading across his palm. Aware of the sound of the gravel shifting beneath his feet, he expected the man to turn to face him, look into his eyes and remember.

He'd played out the scene a thousand times in the days since he'd made his decision in art association. Since he'd taken the roll of tape from his pocket and wrapped it around the pencil tip, then shrouded it in newspaper. Since he'd asked if he could go for a piss, then crouched in the cubicle to slowly shove the pencil up his arse, then walked back into class like a tin soldier.

Now they would be together again, just the two of them. And the man on the bench would get what was coming. What had been coming for seven years. *Go on brother. You've done it before, no problem. This is the cunt that started all this. Do it right this time and finish it for good.*

The man on the bench looked up as Connolly's shadow stole the sunlight, and he smiled.

"Well fuck me, Alan Connolly. Long time no see."

Alan Connolly felt the sharp tip of the pencil pushing into the palm of his hand behind his back and took a step forward. *Go on brother. Straight in his fucking neck. No surrender. No fucking surrender.*

Connolly waited for the familiar surge of electricity, the blinding flashes of white light in his brain that would propel him forward to give Garnett Walsh what he had coming, what he deserved. *Do it Alan. He started this. You can end it now.*

Alan Connolly closed his eyes and felt his heartbeat begin to slow and his breathing normalise as the electrical current grew weaker.

"How's it going Garnett?" Connolly squeezed the pencil and felt the sticky blood in his palm as he placed it back in the pocket of his overalls.

"Apart from being in here mate, yeah I'm alright. What do you know then Alan Connolly?" Garnett Walsh stood up and extended his hand.

Alan Connolly wiped the blood onto his overalls and gripped Garnett Walsh's hand and looked into his eyes.

"What do I know? I'm not sure I know anything for certain anymore pal."

Garnet Walsh laughed and lowered himself back onto the bench. Alan Connolly took his place alongside him and the two men sat in silence, their faces tilted skywards to enjoy a rare moment of natural light amidst the dark stone walls of the prison.

Alan Connolly spat into his blood-stained palm and clenched his fist.

"Actually Garnett, I do know something."

"Yeah? What's that then man?" Garnett Walsh closed his eyes and smiled as the sun escaped a cloud and briefly illuminated his features.

Alan Connolly looked up into the white west Leeds sky and felt the whip of easterly wind sting his cheek. The hum of electricity fell silent and his brother's mocking laughter was lost to the breeze blowing across the exercise yard.

Alan Connolly nodded his head. Still wired wrong. He sensed Garnett Walsh shifting on the bench beside him, now turning to face him.

"What do you know then, Alan Connolly?"

Alan Connolly stood and placed his hand on Walsh's shoulder.

"It doesn't matter anymore. You look after yourself Garnett."

Alan Connolly put his hands in the pockets of his overalls and began to walk across the yard into the wind which whipped the dust from the yard into his eyes.

"Mad Alan! You always were a mystery..." Garnett Walsh laughed and shouted after him. Alan Connolly paused and rubbed at his eyes with his knuckles, then slowly turned to face Walsh.

"Okay Garnett...here's one thing that I do know for a fact. Maybe it's the only thing I really know for certain. Remember Paris 75? That European Cup final? Leeds should have won it, fair and square. We were cheated. Robbed. We really were once the champions, the champions of Europe, and no one will ever take that away from us."

# More books by Billy Morris available in all Amazon stores—

## Bournemouth 90

It's April 1990 and the world is changing. Margaret Thatcher clings to power in the face of poll tax protests, prison riots and sectarian violence in Northern Ireland. The Berlin wall has fallen, South Africa's Apartheid government is crumbling and in the Middle East Saddam Hussein is flexing his muscles, while Iran is still trying to behead Salman Rushdie. In Leeds, United are closing in on a long-awaited return to the first division. Neil Yardsley is heading home after three years away and hoping to go straight. That's the plan, but Neil finds himself being drawn back into a world of football violence and finds a brother up to his neck in the drug culture of the rave scene. Dark family secrets bubble to the surface as Neil tries to help his brother dodge a gangland death sentence, while struggling to keep his own head above water in a city that no longer feels like home. The pressure is building with all roads leading to the south coast, and a final reckoning on a red-hot Bank Holiday weekend in Bournemouth that no one will ever forget.

### Amazon Reviews of Bournemouth 90-

"Fast paced, unflinching read."

"Well researched, 'in the know' story."

"Earthy, Leeds-based, Guy Ritchie style underworld thriller."

"The timeline & atmosphere around the build-up and description of that weekend captures just what it was like to be there."

## LS92

Two years have passed, but the events of Bournemouth 90 continue to cast a dark shadow over the lives of everyone who travelled south on that hot Bank Holiday weekend. Max Jackson is out of jail and trying to re-establish himself in a Leeds underworld being torn apart by gangland warfare. The Yardsley brothers are still paying the price for their actions, with the spectre of Alan Connolly continuing to haunt them. At Millgarth, Sergeant Andy Barton finds himself in the limelight after Bournemouth, but terrace culture is changing, and police intelligence is struggling to adapt to the new normal of the nineties. At Elland Road, a resurgent United are heading towards their first league title in eighteen years, but a disturbing, malevolent force is threatening to gatecrash the champions' victory party. Old scores are settled and new ones imagined, as the climax to the title showdown becomes a deadly quest for vengeance, forgiveness and redemption. LS92. Dark crime fiction from a time when it was still grim up north.

### Amazon Reviews of LS92-

"Fast moving crime thriller which picks up the pace two years on from Bournemouth 90, and captures the changing skyline of 1992 inner city Leeds, with its unforgiving streets, dubious bars and the unique characters of its time."

"If you like crime thrillers with a touch of terrace culture you will enjoy the journey this book takes you on."

"What can you say about a book that you read cover to cover in one session? There's almost no higher praise than that."

"LS92, the sequel to Bournemouth 90 is simply gripping from start to finish."

# LS65

It's Spring 1965, and young Alan Connolly is a man with a plan. Out of jail and out of Glasgow, leaving old wars behind and hoping that the voices in his head allow him to forget the past. New start, new city. Smart suit, the best scooter and the right connections. LS1 is swinging - Coffee bars and clubs, pills and protection rackets. And at Elland Road, Revie's United are chasing a league and cup double in their first season back in the top flight. It's the right place and the perfect time to build his empire and the only thing that can stop him is his own dangerous ambition and the dark memories that torment him.

## Amazon Reviews of LS65-

"Morris's usual heady mix of dark gritty menace, the underworld, and football set against a convincing background of the time – a culture of coffee bars and clubs, drugs and dance halls, Mods and scooters."

"Seamlessly blending fact & fiction, Morris once again draws on his great knowledge of the Leeds story- its subculture, its streets, bars & clubs, its characters, its prejudices, but most of all its football team."

"Great read, especially for anyone who's familiar with Leeds and its streets. I devoured it and finished it within 24 hours."

"Another brilliant novel by a very talented author. It is easy reading, all-action, and very entertaining. I read it in two sittings and loved it!"

"What Morris has established through his previous books is a winning formula. And as the saying goes, 'if it ain't broke, don't fix it' and LS65 doesn't disappoint."

## Birdsong on Holbeck Moor

Autumn 1918. The Great War is drawing to an end and the troops are coming home. The Leeds Pals who survived the carnage of the Somme are returning to a city in the grip of a deadly pandemic, food rationing and unemployment.
In Armley, a war hero needs one more big score to settle a crippling underworld debt, but his illicit wartime schemes are over and time is running out for Frank Holleran and his family. Wartime champions Leeds City FC find themselves in the eye of a financial storm and are struggling to remain a footballing force as the full league resumes. Sports reporter Edgar Rowley is diverted from Elland Road to track an occult animal killer, while helping his brother to overcome his battlefield demons. 1919 is set to be a momentous year, but for some in Leeds, the consequences of their past actions will mean that it's never going to be peaceful. Dark, World War 1 crime fiction from the year that the City became United.

## Amazon Reviews of Birdsong on Holbeck Moor-

"Refreshingly different- dark, fast-paced, with short, snappy chapters that allow the story to flow from many different perspectives."

"Thoroughly researched and well written"

"As ever the writing is tight within this book and Morris manages to juggle the various plotlines effectively."

"There are heroes and villains in this book but not in the clichéd way you find in other crime novels."

"For those that know the Leeds story - and that we've been cursed for years...then this is where our soul begins, the first stamp of our DNA."

Printed in Great Britain
by Amazon